HOODED DETECTIVE

January 1942 Issue

(Volume 3, Number 2)

HOODED DETECTIVE #4
(March 1932)

Pulp Classics #15
Series editor: John Gregory Betancourt

New elements copyright © 2006 by Wildside Press.

Published by:

Wildside Press, LLC
www.wildsidepress.com

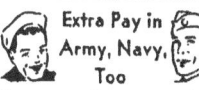

3

FEATURING THE BLACK HOOD!!!
MAN OF MYSTERY!!

HOODED DETECTIVE

VOL. III, No. 2   JANUARY, 1942

A SMASHING BLACK HOOD NOVEL

SIX ACTION PACKED SHORT STORIES

TWO TRUE FACT DETECTIVE SHORTS

HOODED DETECTIVE, published every other month by COLUMBIA PUBLICATIONS, INC. 1
Appleton Street, Holyoke, Mass. Editorial and executive offices 60 Hudson Street, New York, N. Y.
Application for entry as second class matter pending at the Post Office at Holyoke, Mass. Yearly
subscription 60c, single copy 10c. Printed in the U. S. A.

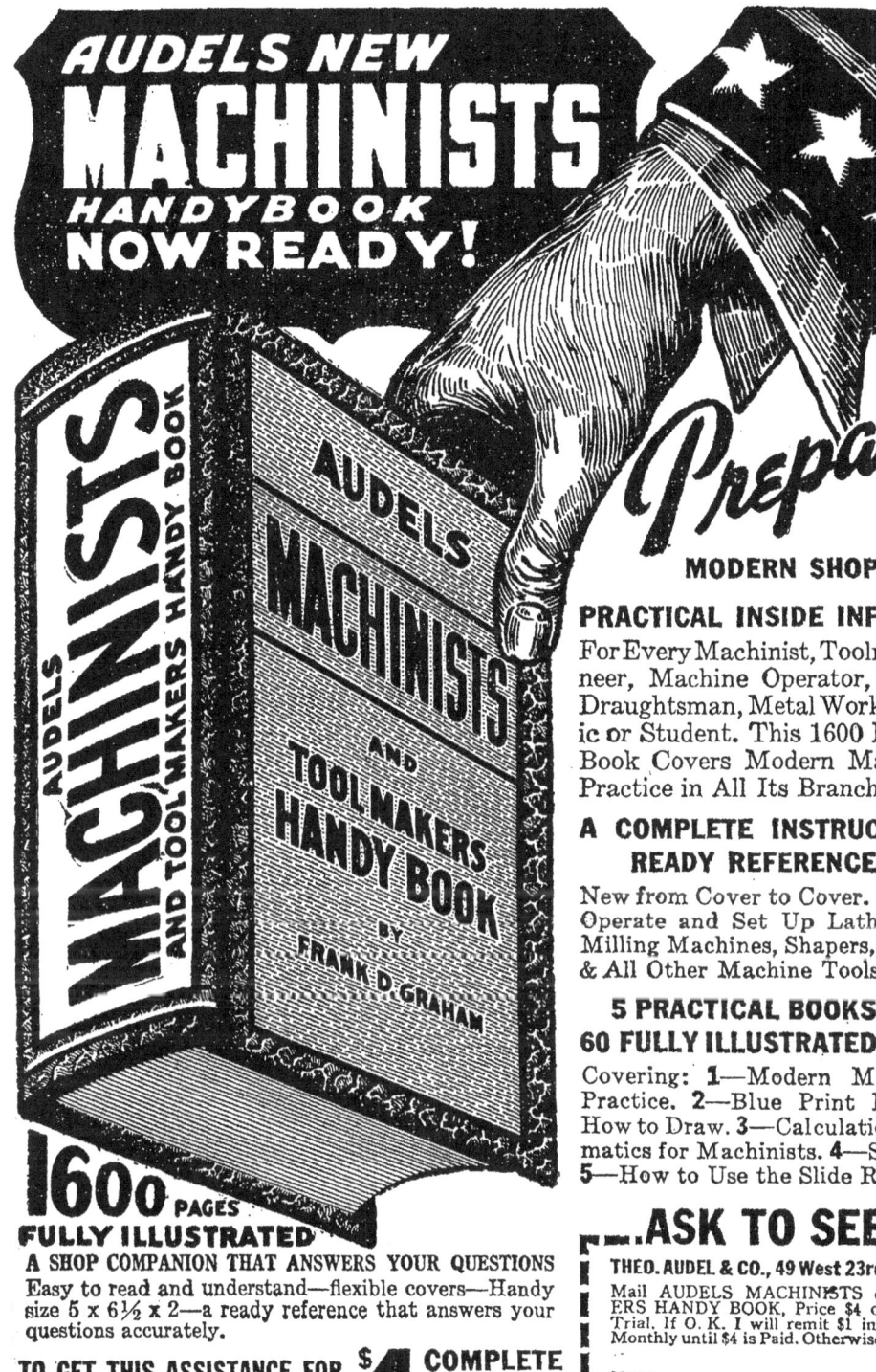
5

7

THE WHISPERING EYE

A BRAND NEW BLACK HOOD NOVEL
by G. T. FLEMING - ROBERTS

Gray jets of live steam erupted from pipes around the edge of the room which threatened to boil BLACK HOOD alive.

CHAPTER I

Rob And Kill

THAT night, the sounds that came from the metal stamping plant of Weedham Industries, Incorporated, might have been prophetic of the immediate and ugly future, for they were like the rattle of machine guns. But Joseph, keeper of the south gate, was blissfully ignorant of a Thompson gun and its deadly chatter, so that he drew no such comparison. His only worry at the time lay in the dark sky above and the blue-white stabs of lightning that promised an electrical storm.

Hunted by the police . . . . framed for robbery and murder by the EYE, master fiend and vicious ruler of the underworld . . . . loathed by Barbara Sutton, the girl who loves him . . . . The BLACK HOOD had to face the blazing purgatory of this murder master's guns to win back Barbara's love and clear himself of the framed charges.

He hated storms. Probably he hated the idea of being murdered, or would have if it ever occurred to him. But then he didn't know that he was going to be murdered, and he did know it was going to storm. The thunder was the tocsin of the storm, but those who came to rob and kill moved unheralded in swift silence.

The night shift had clocked in over an hour ago, and there should be no passing through the gate for at least six hours. Joseph tilted his chair back against the steel fence and kindled his cob pipe. The air was hot and still so that blobs of pipe smoke clung like earth-bound ghosts about him. In spite of the impending storm, Joseph was happy. In his mind was a kindly thought for William "Old Bill" Weedham, principal owner of Weedham Industries. That was because of the bonus Joseph was anticipating.

Within the next twenty-four hours, Joseph knew, seventy-five thousand dollars would be distributed in cash bonuses to the employees of the metal stamping division. Joseph had mentally spent his tiny fraction of the money a dozen times or more. He did a lot of dreaming, Joseph did. But about pleasant things. He had never dreamed of those who rob and kill.

A low slung maroon roadster came down the street and nosed into the mouth of the tarvia drive at Joseph's gate. Joseph eased his chair forward, stood up, approached the car, his faded eyes squinted against the glare of the floodlights mounted on top of the high fence. The car looked like the one young Jeff Weedham drove. Jeff Weedham was "Old Bill" Weedham's son. He took no interest in his father's business or in anything else unless it was that newspaper business which the elder Weedham had purchased for him.

Yes, that was Jeff Weedham at the wheel, and beside him were two other young people—a girl and a redheaded man. Joseph took off his cap and a grin cracked his weathered face.

"Hi," Jeff Weedham said. He was a narrow-headed man with frail-looking sloped shoulders and a thin triangle of face. He had an engaging, careless grin, and light brown eyes that laughed. He had a marked tendency to stutter.

"Well," Joseph said, highly pleased, "if it ain't Mr. Jeff Weedham!"

Joseph sent a shy glance toward the other occupants of the car. The girl instantly reminded him of honey and violets. Hers was one of those clear, golden complexions, and there was a certain unspoiled sweetness about her mouth. It must have been her eyes that recalled violets.

The man on the girl's right seemed to overlap her possessively which could have been accounted for by the width of his shoulders. His red hair bristled in defiance to any comb. His nose looked as though it had been hit a few times in its owner's lifetime. The greenish suit he wore was filled to capacity with overly developed muscles. A leather cased camera was suspended from his bull neck by means of a strap. He had a flashlight gun in his right hand, and a photographer's tripod was propped upright between his knees.

"D-d-do you think you could let us in?" Jeff Weedham asked of Joseph. "*The D-Daily Opinion* is going to give D-d-dad a plug."

The Daily Opinion was the newspaper which Bill Weedham had bought for his son, Joseph recalled.

"Why, I guess so," Joseph replied. "But your friends here will have to sign the register book."

The big redhead had some difficulty getting into the pocket of his suit coat from which he extracted a card. He swelled importantly as he handed it across to the gate keeper. The card read, "*The Daily Opinion.* Joe Strong, News Photographer."

He said, "I guess this will fix everything, huh Jeff?"

"This is Miss Barbara Sutton," Jeff said, indicating the girl beside him. "I've hired her as a reporter, and Joe Strong is her cameraman. I just came along to see that they get inside. They're d-d-doing an article on the various manufacturing plants around New York."

JOSEPH bowed to Barbara Sutton. "You folks can go right in, just as soon as you sign the book." He went back to his post and returned with a ledger. He turned pages with a moistened thumb, took a pencil out of his pocket, passed both to the passengers of the roadster. Barbara Sutton and Joe Strong signed.

"Looks like it's kicking up a storm," Joseph said.

The thunder rolled ominous reply to his remark. Then Joseph went to the gate, opened it, and the roadster rolled up the drive toward the stamping mill.

Joseph went back to his chair and re-kindled his pipe. He smiled at the memory of Barbara Sutton. He didn't know when he had seen a prettier girl. There must be an awful lot of young fellows who thought the same thing.

"And if I was twenty years younger I

guess I'd try to give them a lot of competition!" he said aloud and chuckled.

His chuckle stopped as lightning flare threw the shadow of a man across the ground at Joseph's feet. He looked up, startled. The man faced Joseph silently. He was slight, wore a workman's overall suit, and he had a lunch box under his arm. His face, what could be seen of it beneath the low drawn hat, was one of starved cheeks, lipless mouth, pinched nose, and a chin that seemed to dangle.

Joseph at first thought the man was one of the mill hands who had arrived late for work.

"You don't care what time you show up," Joseph grumped. "You know you're over an hour late?"

The slight man laughed unpleasantly.

"I ain't late," he said. "I guess I'm just about in time."

Something with the glint of bright steel flashed from the lunch box under the man's arm. Instantly Joseph's mind connected this with the seventy-five thousand dollars in small bills that was to come in on the bank express truck in a few minutes.

Stick-up! Joseph's brain shrieked the alarm. He tried to get out of his chair, but a knife blade that was like a sliver of light was driven into Joseph's throat, sliding through flesh and muscle, torturing every pain nerve in his body, driving relentlessly until the point of it wedged into the wood back of the gate keeper's chair.

The chair creaked and groaned beneath Josephs' writhings. But the knife and the thin, dirty fingers of the killer did not permit his body to alter its position. And then the pain nerves died. Joseph's brain emptied, fortunately; a man would not want to know that he was tacked to a chair, bleeding to death.

The killer released Joseph. A little of the spurting blood had got on his dirty fingers, and he wiped his hands on the seat of his trousers. Then he removed the keys from the gate keeper's pocket. He went to the gate, unlocked it, and opened it wide.

There were great overgrown shrubs on either side of the gate just outside the factory grounds. The killer walked to the bushes at the west side of the gate, parted the branches with his dirty fingers.

"Delancy," his voice croaked.

The shrubbery shook. The thick torso of a man who squatted like a toad could be seen partly emerging from the shrubs.

"Okay, Shiv?"

"Okay, Delancy," the killer chuckled. "His own mudder would t'ink he was asleep in the chair. Don't death make a guy look natural, huh?"

"You get back to the car," the man in the bushes said. "Be ready to pick us up as soon as we crack the money truck. If you get nervous, think of the dough. Seventy-five grand!"

"I ain't noivous!" the killer said. "T'ink I never croaked a guy before. It's a pipe. Dis whole job is a pipe, wit' us havin' a Monitor gun to open dat armored truck. I'm almost ashamed to be associated wit' such a pipe of a job."

"Sure it's a pipe," Delancy agreed from amid the bushes. "Only don't get too cocky on account of there's one guy who could mess things up for us if he ever hits our trail."

Shiv laughed. "You're worrying about the Black Hood, huh?"

"I'm not worrying," Delancy said crossly. "I'm just being cautious. Each job we do for the boss gets a little bigger. One of these times we'll run into Mr. Black Hood."

"And when we do—" the killer drew a line across his throat with his forefinger. Then he turned and walked away from the bushes.

ᴅELANCY'S moon face disappeared in the foliage. Only his hard little eyes glittered in the shadows. Beside him, patiently silent, was Squid Murphy. Murphy was motionless except for his twitching left eyelid. Murphy was manning the Colt Monitor rifle, the kind of gun the G-men used to death-drill the armor plate cars the mobsters sometimes used. Tonight the weapon was in other hands.

Delancy watched the lean figure of the knifeman ambling leisurely up the road toward where the get-away car was parked, lights out. Shiv wasn't nervous. Neither was Murphy, in spite of his twitching eyelid. There was nothing to be nervous about since they had hooked up with this new boss—this guy Delancy had never seen; this guy who knew all the answers. No, there was nothing to worry about as long as that relentless hunter of criminals known as the Black Hood kept off their tail.

Delancy wasn't nervous even when the

blunt gray snout of the bank express truck turned into the mouth of the drive and slowed up before the open gate. He just took a firmer grip on his automatic and waited.

The driver of the bank trunk yelled at the motionless figure of Joseph. And when Joseph didn't answer, the driver nudged the guard who rode beside him.

"What the hell's wrong with their watchman?"

Delancy heard that. His little eyes saw the guard get out of the cab. He saw that the back door of the armored truck was opening and another guard was getting out. Delancy thought, *What a break this is!* And then he shot the driver in the back.

The guard who had ridden up in front snatched at his shoulder holster as he turned in the direction of Delancy's fire. On the other side of the drive, two more of Delancy's boys opened up with automatics, so that by the time the guard had decided he was facing death, death spoke from behind him. Two slugs ripped into him. His own gun jumped twice, the first shot coming dangerously close to Delancy's head, while the second was an unaimed thing caused by the convulsive jerk of the guard's trigger finger as he spilled forward on his face.

The man who had got out of the rear of the truck saw a glimpse of the hell that had spouted from the shrubbery and tried to duck for cover behind the truck. And beside Delancy, the Monitor gun came to life. It talked fast in a language that was all its own. It got the retreating guard twice, the heavy, bone-shattering slugs knocking the man first one way and then another as he fell crazily to the ground.

There were two guards inside the truck. Their guns roared from the ports in the armored walls. But the Monitor rifle was a can opener. Crouching beside Squid Murphy, Delancy felt the heat of its barrel and saw the black periods that were bullet holes speckling the gray steel sides of the truck. Now only one of the gun ports in the truck was active.

The barrel of the Monitor swung and the hot steel barrel burned Delancy's arm. He said, "Hell!" hoarsely and jumped out of the bushes, automatic in hand. Delancy dropped flat and heard the sound of a bullet whining by. And then the Monitor's deafening hammer sounded again, and after that, silence.

Delancy picked himself up, ran, his thick, toadlike body silhouetted by the truck lights. Gun smoke lay in placidly moving layers of gray before the light beams. Delancy ducked through the open door of the truck. One of his own men was already inside, and he tossed a money bag to Delancy. Delancy caught it with one arm and a belly and passed it back through the door to Squid Murphy who was standing just outside.

Delancy said, "Cut it, Murphy!" Because Squid Murphy was giggling. Murphy was kill-crazy, and tonight the Monitor rifle in his hands had made him feel like a god. His giggling rasped on Delancy's nerves.

Delancy picked up another money bag, and then told his boys they'd have to get going. He didn't know why he felt as though they ought to get away in a hurry. Surely no one inside the Weedham plant could have heard the gun fire above the racket the machines were making. Also, the neighborhood about the factory was thinly populated.

But something he couldn't put his finger on was spurring Delancy to get clear of the scene of the crime as soon as possible. Maybe it was the lightning that flashed with ever increasing frequency. Or maybe it was the ghastly tableau the body of Joseph, the watchman, made, sitting in that chair, pinned there like a butterfly by Shiv's knife.

A big gray sedan stood in the middle of the road, the motor idling. Shiv the knifeman slouched indolently behind the wheel. Murphy and the other two gunmen were already getting into the rear seat, and Delancy went cold with the sudden fear that his pals might run out on him. As fast as his short bowed legs would carry him, he ran to the car and piled in beside Shiv. The knifeman looked at Delancy and snickered.

"What's the rush, Delancy? You think Black Hood is on your tail?"

Delancy snarled, "Hell, no! But let's get going, huh?"

Now that Shiv had mentioned it, Delancy recognized the fear that plagued him. It was fear of the Black Hood. The Black Hood wasn't like the cops at all. He didn't trail a man with screaming sirens and blasting whistles. He hunted like a panther in the night, alone and silent. And you never knew just when the shadow of this master manhunter was to fall across your path.

CHAPTER II

Secret Traffic

IF DELANCY had stayed a little longer at the scene of his crime, he would have learned that his premonition was founded in truth. The Black Hood *was* hard on Delancy's heels that night. Advance notice of the stick-up at the Weedham plant had sifted up through the underworld grapevine to come eventually to Black Hood's ears. It had been very scanty information and late in its arrival—too late to enable the master manhunter to block the plan. All that Black Hood had learned was that robbery of the Weedham factory had been planned, which wasn't anything very definite considering that the Weedham Industries occupied over fifty acres of ground.

When all hell broke loose at the south gate of the factory, Black Hood was actually at the north-west corner of the grounds. A cat could scarcely have seen him, lurking in the shadows, his tall figure shrouded in a black silk cape, his head and face hidden by his famous hood. But his position did give him one advantage over those actually at work in the factory buildings—he could distinguish the rattle of gun fire from the racket made by the stamping mill.

At the sound of the first shot, Black Hood had climbed to the top of the high wire fence to leap into the factory grounds. Lightning had seen him streaking through the open areas between buildings—a weird figure in yellow tights, night-black shorts and hooded mask, his cape whipping out from his broad shoulders. He might have been mistaken for a man from Mars or a devil out of Hell, yet beneath the grotesque garb beat a heart that was warm and human.

Black Hood knew what it was to be a policeman with hands bound by red tape or political intrigue. He knew what it was to be a criminal, to be hunted as Delancy was hunted. Once he had been a young cop, determined to work his way up in the police force. One of the most diabolical fiends of the underworld had framed this cop for a crime. The frame had stuck. In his efforts to clear himself, the young cop had taken half a dozen lead slugs from underworld guns into his body. He had been left on a lonely mountain road, apparently dead, later to be found by that wise, gray-whiskered man known as the Hermit.

It was the Hermit's vast store of scientific knowledge that brought the half-dead cop back to health. It was the Hermit who gave the ex-cop a body with the strength of steel and a mind that was a veritable encyclopedia of scientific knowledge. It was the Hermit who had sent the ex-cop back into the world to live a useful life, to strike back at the denizens of the underworld who had harmed him.

So the Black Hood was born to live in two identities. By day he was a pleasant, mild-mannered young man known as Kip Burland to Barbara Sutton, Joe Strong, and others of their set. But at night Kip Burland became the Black Hood, man of mystery, hunter of killers. Police who did not understand the unorthodox methods of the Black Hood suspected him of numerous crimes. The underworld that feared him wanted him dead. He was the hunter hunted.

Once the secret of his dual identity became known, he knew that he faced either death from the hands of criminals or prison from the hands of police. Barbara Sutton, who merely tolerated Kip Burland, was deeply in love with the Black Hood, yet even Barbara did not know that Kip and the Black Hood were one and the same person.

Black Hood was not the only person at the Weedham plant who had heard the gun fire at the south gate. Joe Strong, newly appointed cameraman on Jeff Weedham's newspaper, had been standing at one of the doors of the stamping mill, smoking a cigarette when the hold-up had taken place. However, it required a few seconds for his dull brain to comprehend just what was taking place and from what direction the shots had come.

Joe Strong had been trying to develop a nose for news. When he finally realized what was going on at the south gate, he decided that here was a chance for some swell pictures that would prove to Jeff Weedham and Barbara Sutton that he was a natural born news hound. He ran from the stamping mill, his camera bobbing from the strap around his neck and his tripod dragging behind him. He had heard that a crack news photographer could adjust a camera on the run and he figured that he could do that and also mount the camera on the tripod at the same time.

It was a very good idea except that like most of the ideas that sprouted slowly from Joe's brain, it didn't work. He was within fifteen yards of the scene of the crime when he tripped over one leg of his tripod and fell flat on his face.

WHEN he picked himself up, he saw something that knocked all ideas of picture taking out of his thick skull. A brilliant blaze of lightning showed him the unmistakable figure of the Black Hood bending over the body of Joseph, the watchman. He saw Black Hood's gauntlet gloved hand closed on the handle of the knife that was thrust into Joseph's neck.

Joe Strong had met Black Hood many times before, and, like the police, Joe was convinced that Black Hood was a clever criminal. It occurred to Joe in the darkness that followed the lightning flash, that it was Black Hood who had stuck up the bank truck, slaughtered the guards, and was just now in the act of finishing off Joseph, the only remaining witness to his crime.

So natural was the position of old Joseph in his chair that Black Hood, too, had made the mistake of thinking that the watchman was alive. He had approached Joseph with the idea of learning something about the escaping criminals. He turned, now, from the murdered gate keeper to see Joe Strong bearing down upon him, fists balled, square teeth showing, his wide, coarse-featured face a mask of determination. He knew that Joe Strong, in spite of his clumsiness, could be a nasty opponent in a scrap.

Joe closed in fast, led with his left fist in a blow that began way down and ended exactly nowhere—nowhere, because Black Hood side-stepped both the haymaker and Joe Strong.

"Gangway, muscle man!" Black Hood's voice rang out, and then like a slim arrow unleashed from a taut drawn bow Black Hood sped up the tarvia drive toward where the low slung roadster that belonged to Jeff Weedham was parked.

Black Hood vaulted into the roadster without bothering to open the door. Jeff Weedham had left the key in the ignition lock. The black gauntlet covered fingers of the master manhunter gave the key a twist and at the same time he plugged in the starter button. The motor responded instantly. Black Hood brought the car around in a wide sweeping turn to head back toward the gate, had to swerve to avoid hitting Joe Strong.

There were some of the admirable qualities of the bull dog about Joe Strong. Once his one-track mind got to functioning on a certain objective it seldom digressed. And at the present moment his was determined to stop Black Hood. As the roadster passed, straightening out of its loop turn, Joe leaped to the running board, seized the wheel in one hand and tried to get Black Hood by the throat with the other. The car left the drive as Joe yanked at the wheel. It bounded toward a round bed of evergreens that beautified the factory grounds. Black Hood released the wheel, stood up on the pedals, and at the same time slammed Joe across the face with the back of his gauntlet covered left hand. The blow, the sudden stopping of the car, combined effectively to give Joe the shake. He went backwards, sailing through the air, to land in the evergreen bed.

Black Hood let the clutch slap in and the roadster bounded back onto the tarvia drive. Perhaps none but the steel-nerved Black Hood would have tried to get through that factory gate, partially blocked as it was by the crippled bank truck. But the master manhunter could have driven a gas truck through Hell's own fire. Instead of slowing the car to squeeze through the narrow opening, he tramped on the gas pedal and set his teeth for the shock he knew was coming. Because he knew that the space between truck and gate post was too narrow to allow the roadster to pass unscarred.

The right front fender hit the brick of the gate post. There was a scream of tortured metal as the fender was sheared from the body. The impact dragged down on the speed of the roadster so that the rear right fender was only crumpled by the brick work. But momentum was sufficient to carry Jeff Weedham's roadster out onto the road.

Black Hood knew that the criminals had taken the road toward town. As soon as he had reached the south gate he had ascertained this by a glance at the gravel shoulder of the road. Whoever had been driving the get-away car had started in a hurry so that one rear wheel threw gravel in the opposite direction of travel. Just how much of a lead the rob and kill men had on him, Black Hood did not know. But he did knew that Jeff Weedham's car was a gallant piece of machinery, capable of tremendous speed and so nicely balanced that it could cling to sharp curves.

ACTUALLY, only a few seconds had elapsed between the, time when Delancy and his killers had hit the road and the time when Black Hood had arrived at the south gate. The man called Shiv was driving Delancy's get-away car at a conservative pace so as not to excite suspicion. In this Shiv showed more wisdom than did Delancy.

"You think you're going to a funeral?" Delancy demanded when his patience could endure the pace no longer.

Shiv said, "But you'll be goin' to one if I open dis crate up. You want speed cops on your tail, Delancy?"

"To hell with the cops," Delancy snarled. "Step it up a little."

Shiv speeded up to forty miles an hour as he rolled to the top of a little hill. A mile or so distant the lights of one of New York's suburbs twinkled in the darkness.

"We got lots of time," Shiv said. "You're noivous, Delancy. You got ants. Up here at this next town we slide into a filling station and get us a new paint job and new plates, all in the space of ten minutes. Like I said before, dis job is a pipe."

Delancy didn't hear Shiv. He was twisted around in the front seat, looking over the heads of Squid Murphy and the two other gunsels in the back seat. Through the rear window, Delancy saw twin swords of light from the lamps of another car not so far behind them.

"We're tailed now," he said hoarsely.

"Aw nuts!" Murphy said from the back seat. "We ought to make you get out and walk. Every time you see a car behind you, you get the ants."

Delancy drew his tongue over dry lips. He said, "Take a look for yourself, Murphy. That guy behind is burning asphalt off the road."

Murphy and the other hoods looked backwards. The car behind was a roadster, they could see in a sudden splash of lightning. And it was traveling like the wind.

Delancy opened the glove compartment in the instrument board and took out a pair of field glasses. He got to his knees on the front seat, turned around so that he could sight out the back window. He tried to hold the speeding roadster in the range of the glasses, and when the lightning came again he thought he could make out the figure of the driver at the wheel. He thought that he saw a sleek rounded head closely covered by a black silk hood. He was almost certain that he saw a black silk cape whipping out from the shoulders of the lone man in the car.

Delancy got cold all over. He gripped Shiv's shoulder convulsively, nearly sending his own car into the ditch by so doing.

"Step on it, Shiv," he said hoarsely. "I don't like. the looks of that guy in the car behind us."

"So you don't like the guy's hair-do!" Shiv sneered. "And I should kick the bottom out of dis crate just because you don't like the looks of somebody behind us!"

Delancy passed the glasses back to Squid Murphy.

"See what you see, Murphy," he said quietly. Then he turned around, hauled out his gun, and shoved it into Shiv's ribs. "When I said step on it, I wasn't fooling."

"Gees!" Murphy said. "That guy back there's got a hell of a thing on his head. Looks like a hood."

"A black hood," Delancy said. "And I don't think I want to have anything to do with that guy, do you, Shiv?"

Shiv came down on the gas pedal and the car picked up speed. He said, "All right, all right! I'm steppin' on it, ain't I?"

If Delancy's car hadn't speeded up, Black Hood in the car behind might not have taken particular notice of it. But that sudden spurt of speed on the part of the gray sedan was a dead give-away. Black Hood knew that he was hot on the trail.

The big gray sedan carrying Delancy and his pals, hit the suburban town at a scant seventy miles an hour. It ran by three red lights without shaking the roadster piloted by Black Hood. The streets were slippery with rain that was sheeting out of the black sky, and when Shiv tried to negotiate the next corner, the big sedan turned completely around.

Delancy thought then that the chase was over, but Shiv had a trick or two up his sleeve. He spurted, took the car half way down the block, heading in the very direction from which Black Hood was coming. Then Shiv whipped his wheel around for a short turn into the mouth of an alley.

Delancy breathed again. He could see where everything was going to be all right now. The gray sedan bounced over the rough alley pavement, cut across the street at the next block, and rolled onto the concrete area in front of a large gas service station. The overhead doors beneath a sign which advertised car washing by steam ran up on their track as the gray sedan came into sight. Shiv steered into the wash room, and the doors dropped back into place.

Delancy got out, his body bathed in a cold sweat. The proprietor of this gas station was in the employ of Delancy's boss who had planned every step of the stick-up at the Weedham plant and the subsequent get-away. Delancy had supreme faith in his boss. For the first time since he had sighted that strange figure in the roadster that had followed them, he began to feel a little bit secure.

Delancy entered the filling station office, followed by his mob. The proprietor, a huge bear of a man in brown coveralls, scowled at Delancy. He said:

"The way you came in here, it's a wonder you didn't bring a whole squad of cops with you. What's the matter, anyway?"

Delancy didn't answer just then. The proprietor of the station wasn't alone in his office. There was a dame. She was a tall, well-dressed woman with wax-pale skin and black hair that was parted in the middle and slicked back to a soft knot. She had peculiarly cold green eyes that were tilted at the outer extremities. Her lips were full, soft and brilliantly rouged.

Delancy jerked his head at the woman and asked of the proprietor: "Who's that, Burkey?"

Burkey shrugged big shoulders. "She's from the boss. She's got a message for you."

The woman was beautiful. But there was something about the chilly expression in her eyes that made Delancy feel decidedly uncomfortable. She did not smile as she opened a black purse and produced an envelope which she handed to Delancy.

While Burkey was opening the steam valves that would spray hot vapor on the car in the wash room, Delancy tore open the letter which the woman had handed him. Inside was a slip of paper on which had been typed the following:

"The bearer will ride with you into Manhattan."

There was no signature, but in its stead was the crude drawing of an eye, formed by two bowed lines that represented lids and two circles, one within the other, representing iris and pupil. Delancy knew that the message was from that man he had never seen—the big boss, the man who knew all the answers.

Delancy touched a match to the message. He looked at the woman with the cold green eyes.

"What's the idea?" he asked.

"I suppose," she said in a quiet voice, "that it will look less suspicious if you are seen driving a car with a woman beside you. Your men are to get into the baggage trunk at the rear or else crouch down on the floor of the rear compartment."

Delancy snorted. "That's nuts. There ain't any sense to this. It was a clean job. We didn't mix with any coppers."

"No?" she said, elevating her eyebrows. "Nevertheless, you will carry out the orders. The Eye knows what he's doing."

CHAPTER III

Haven Of The Hunted

TEN minutes later, Delancy drove the get-away car out of the service station. It was a gray sedan no longer. It was a brilliant blue job with red wheels, and it carried a Texas license. Delancy was at the wheel and the woman with the cold green eyes rode beside him. Two of Delancy's gunmen crouched out of sight on the floor of the rear compartment while two more had been crowded into the luggage compartment at the rear.

As the car rolled on toward Manhattan's northern boundary, the woman with the green eyes switched on the radio on the dash. All of the cars used on stick-up jobs were furnished with receivers capable of picking up police calls, and out of the corner of his eye, Delancy saw that the woman was twisting the dial down to the police band.

"What's the idea?" Delancy asked. He wasn't particularly pleasant to this woman who rode with him, largely because she treated him like the dirt under her feet.

"I simply want to check up," she said coldly. "I want to know just how clean that job was."

"Clean?" Delancy fumed. "Listen, lady, we knocked off every damned guy who could have told anything about us. And there wasn't a copper in sight. Why, I haven't seen a bull in so long I'd have to look twice to recognize one."

"That may be," she admitted, "but I want to make sure."

"Listen," Delancy said, now thoroughly angry, "how do you get that way? Who the hell are you, checking up on me? You the Eye's moll?"

"Moll?" questioned the woman. "I do not understand."

"You don't understand!" Delancy scoffed. "Listen, babe, don't get high-hat with me or I'll slap you down."

"You would not be so foolish," she said scornfully. "The Eye would tear you into small pieces. He would—"

The flat voice of a police announcer came from the radio speaker and interrupted the threat:

"Warning to all cars. Be on the lookout for blue Buick sedan, nineteen thirty-nine model, red wheels, being driven by Raymond Delancy. Delancy is wanted for hold-up and murder. Wanted for hold-up and murder, Ray Delancy, height five feet eight inches, weighing one hundred eighty pounds—"

Delancy's hand shot out to the radio switch, cutting off the voice of the announcer. It was impossible! There had been no police at the Weedham plant. No cops had tailed them. No cops had seen that the gray sedan which had driven into Burkey's filling station had come out a blue sedan.

"A clean job, you said?" the woman with the green eyes mocked.

One of the gunmen who crouched on the floor of the rear compartment cursed quietly and without interruption for nearly a minute. Delancy tramped nervously on the gas pedal.

"Don't worry, anybody," he said. "The heat's on, and I don't know how the hell the cops got that way, but it ain't the first time I've give them the shake. We'll go to Jack Carlson's garage. He'll get us out of this. It'll cost something, but hell, we've got lots of dough."

Delancy drove as though he was rolling on thin ice. The sight of a traffic cop made him dodge around a corner that threw him off his course. He came close to having convulsions when a squad car passed on the next street west, its siren wailing. He told the boys in the back seat to get their guns out, just in case they had to shoot it out. But somehow all of his anxiety was wasted, and he at last sighted a neon sign which read:

"ATLAS AUTO LIVERY"

Delancy turned the sedan through the door of the big garage, rolled across the wide parking floor to the cement ramp at the rear. He got into second gear and zoomed up the ramp to the second floor. Then he got out of the car, walked to the office which was partitioned off from the rest of the floor by means of frosted glass. The door of the office carried the words, "Jack Carlson, President."

Carlson had started out as the operator of a wildcat bus company. In this business he had learned so many ways to circumvent the law that he had decided to put that knowledge to more lucrative uses. Under the cover of a legitimate auto livery and trucking business, he had built a vast transportation system which was employed by any criminal who was wanted by the police and could afford to pay Carlson's fee. When the town got too hot for a killer or stick-up artist, Jack Carlson had many tricks up his sleeve which would enable the wanted man to move to a cooler spot.

DELANCY entered Carlson's reception room which was never closed. At the invitation of the blonde stenographer at the desk, he squatted on a chair and lighted a cigarette. Jack Carlson entered the room a moment later, walking with the energetic bounce of a busy man.

Carlson was a little above medium height, dark complexioned, his brow a washboard of horizontal wrinkles. He had a waxed mustache which he was in the habit of twisting whenever in deep thought.

"Well, well, well," he said cheerfully as he shook hands with Delancy. "Some little trouble bothering you tonight, Ray?"

Delancy scowled. He couldn't see that there was anything to be cheerful about.

"The boys and I pulled a little job," he said. "It didn't amount to a whole lot, but I think there's a leak somewhere in our organization. The cops got the heat on us, and we'd like a hand out of town for a few days."

Carlson went to his desk, sat down, stuck a slim cigar in his well formed lips.

"How much was your job?" he asked quietly as he struck a match.

"Not much," Delancy said. "Maybe ten grand at the outside." He purposely lied about the take because Carlson usually charged on the percentage basis. Another thing which was inclined to influence Carlson's price was that little business of murder. If you killed on a job Carlson considered the danger greater and pushed up his fee accordingly.

"Anybody knocked off, Ray?" Jack Carlson asked.

Delancy squirmed uncomfortably in his chair. "One of the boys had to shoot a guard in the leg. Nothing messy, though."

Carlson inhaled deeply. A faint smile came to his lips. He removed his cigar and waved it at Delancy.

"So you got only ten grand, Ray? And nobody knocked off?"

"That's what I said," Delancy crabbed.

Carlson chuckled. "I happen to know that a number of men were killed, that you're wanted for murder, and that your total take was about seventy-five thousand dollars. And it'll cost you just thirty-two thousand five hundred dollars of that money to get you out of the jam."

"Thirty-two thousand—" Delancy gasped.

Carlson waved his cigar. "But for that price I'll see that you and all your boys get a nice cool spot to hideout in, somewhere a long way from New York."

Delancy stood up. "Why you damned greaseball, you! I'd see you in hell first. Pay fifty per cent of my take to you and the usual ten per cent to the Eye for his part of the job! Hell, that leaves me a lousey forty per cent without counting the split to the boys."

"Take it or leave it," Carlson shrugged.

"I'll leave it!" Delancy rapped. "Why, damn you, that's robbery!"

"And your crime was murder," Carlson said. He twisted his mustache thoughtfully. "I think you'll take my offer, Delancy, because there just isn't any other out for you."

Delancy's scowl deepened. His eyes narrowed. An idea was beginning to roll around inside his head. He didn't know

exactly what he ought to do with it, but it was an idea, anyway.

He said, "You think there's no other out for me, huh? Well, I'll make an out before I'll pay any such figure to you. And listen, fellah, if I thought—" He stopped a moment, dropped his cigarette onto the carpet and heeled it out. "Well anyway, Carlson, I'm going to have a little talk with the Eye. And that little talk is going to be about you and the rotten deal you tried to hand me."

"Go ahead and talk," Carlson said. "And when the cops start closing in on you and your mob, let me know. I'll get you out of the jam for the same figure."

Carlson got up, walked around his desk to where Delancy stood in front of the door. He stuck out his hand.

"No hard feelings, Ray?"

Delancy looked down at the hand and sneered.

"No hard feelings, chiseler, but I sure would like to put a couple of slugs in your belly!" And Delancy swaggered out of the office. He guessed he'd told that chiseler where he got off.

As soon as the door had closed, Jack Carlson bounded back to his desk, touched a button on an inter-office communications box. Somebody on the lower floor of the garage answered.

Carlson said, "Ray Delancy is just leaving. I want him tailed."

CHAPTER IV

Live Steam

THE BLACK HOOD had reached a dead-end in the trail which had led him from the Weedham Industries plant. The gray sedan in which the fleeing criminals were riding had vanished, apparently into thin air. Black Hood had spent thirty minutes of search at breakneck speed in an attempt to pick up the trail of the gray sedan again. He had driven the roadster which belonged to Jeff Weedham in and out of alleys in a trial and error effort to sight the killers' car, but all without success.

It occurred to him then that it was entirely possible that the rob and kill boys had not left the suburban town at all. Perhaps this was their hideout. With that in mind, he parked Jeff Weedham's car and stepped out into the rain, his black cape, wrapped around him. He felt that he could walk the streets in comparative safety in spite of his costume, for it would have required close inspection under direct light to distinguish the garb he wore from the standard poncho and rain-hood worn by the traffic police in bad weather.

After an hour or more of leg work that yielded him no information so far as a possible hideout for the criminals was concerned, Black Hood came across the drunk. The drunk was in a dismal alley, leaning up against the wall of a tavern which he had evidently just left. He was a young man, and he wore some sort of a uniform —that of a chauffeur, taxi driver, or something of the sort. When Black Hood put in his appearance, the young man started to move along up the alley, staggering as he walked.

"Wait a minute," Black Hood called.

" 'S all right, officer," the drunk said, mistaking Black Hood for a cop. "I'm on my way. I'm goin' home."

"You think you'll get there, weaving around that way?" Black Hood asked, catching up with the man. "If you don't fall asleep under the wheels of a truck you'll be mighty lucky."

"Only live a block from here," the drunk explained. "I'll make it. I gotta skin full, all right. Never been drunk before, so help me, officer. But Burkey fired me because he said I was drunk when I wasn't. A man's gotta live up to his reputation, don't he?"

"Who's Burkey?" Black Hood asked. He was determined to see that the young drunk got safely home.

"Runs the Super-Charged Gasoline Station two blocks south of here. He said he wouldn't have a drunk working for him, but I was cold sober when it happened."

"When what happened?" Black Hood linked his arm with that of the young man.

"I was out at the gas pumps when a gray sedan barreled into the station and in onto the wash rack," the young man explained. "Burkey brought the doors down in the wash room and turned on the steam. About ten minutes later, the gray sedan drove out the other side of the wash room, and it wasn't gray any more. It was blue —blue with red wheels."

At the mention of a gray sedan traveling fast, Black Hood's interest increased.

"Maybe," he suggested, "there were two cars in the wash room."

"Can't be," the young man said. "There's only room for one at a time. I went to Burkey and asked him how it happened that a car would change color like that. He said it hadn't changed color and if I thought it had I must be drunk. So he fired me. But I was cold sober, I tell you. And I'd like to know what I'm going to do and what my widowed mother is going to do with me out of a job."

Black Hood reached inside his cape. The broad black belt which he wore contained many secret pockets, and from one of these he extracted a ten-dollar bill. He pressed the money into the young man's hand.

"That'll tide you over until you can find a job," he said. "Think you can get across the street all right?"

They had reached the end of the alley by this time, and the young drunk had said that his home was just on the other side of the street. The drunk stared at the crumpled bill in his hand. Then he raised his eyes to Black Hood's face. In the glow from a nearby street lamp he could clearly see the black mask that covered the upper part of Black Hood's face to the tip of his nose. The drunk was startled.

"Who—who are you?" he stammered.

Black Hood laughed. "Never mind, son. Just forget you ever saw me." Then he turned and ran back along the alley to walk quickly in the direction of the gas station where the drunk had worked, two blocks to the south.

The overhead door of the car washing room was open, and as Black Hood entered it he glanced through the glass pane of the door connecting this portion of the service station with the office. A big, shaggy-haired man in brown overalls had just picked up the telephone from his battered, grease-stained desk. This man would be Burkey, the owner of the station.

Black Hood's keen eyes flicked around the room in which he now stood. At the back, near a stand that racked a number of grease guns, he saw a second telephone fixed to the wall. An extension of the one in the office, he wondered?

He crossed to the wall phone and gently removed the receiver from its hook and held it to his ear. He heard a gruff voice which might well have been that of the man Burkey, say: "Is this the Eye?"

BLACK HOOD'S eyes narrowed. The voice that came back over the wire was a toneless whisper.

"This is the Eye speaking."

Burkey said, "Delancy came through here about a couple of hours ago."

"Delancy?" the Eye said. "Yes, I know."

"I changed paint jobs for him according to instructions," Burkey explained. "But what I called you about, I got a young fellow working here, grinding gas. He saw the gray sedan roll in here and he saw that it was blue when it went out. He came to me to ask how come."

"What did you do?" the Eye whispered.

"Told him he was drunk and fired him," Burkey replied.

"That was careless of you," the voice whispered after the pause of a moment. "Very careless. You should have silenced this man at once."

Burkey said, "How the hell could I do that?"

"That is your problem," the whisperer said. "But you must dispose of him immediately, do you understand?"

"Is that an order?"

"That is an order," the Eye whispered grimly, and broke the connection.

Black Hood hung up quietly. Then crouching low, he crossed the room to where the strainer top of the sewer drain was placed in the concrete floor. It was in this room that Delancy's get-away car had changed paint jobs, and in about ten minutes. How was such a thing possible?"

He dropped to his knees, nerves tense as he lifted the strainer plate. Dove gray particles clung to the sewer opening beneath—particles of some sort of paint that was soluble in water or perhaps live steam. A glint of understanding came into his eyes. Delancy had driven the get-away car into this room. The car actually was not a gray car at all. It was a blue car, the paint covered with this gray, steam soluble substance. All that was necessary to convert the car which Black Hood had been following into a blue car which he certainly would have missed was a good bath of steam. It wouldn't have required more than ten minutes at the outside.

A rumbling sound that did not originate in the thunder caps above jerked Black Hood's attention from the drain. His glance darted toward the overhead doors which were dropping swiftly into place. His eyes turned toward the door leading into the service station office. Burkey, the proprietor, was standing at the door, watching Black Hood through the glass. There was a diabolical grin on the face of the station owner.

Black Hood straightened as the overhead doors fell into place and locked. He took two long, springy strides toward the door. But he never quite reached that door. With an explosive hiss, gray jets of live steam erupted from pipes aorund the edge of the room. Scalding steam that could burn and blister and boil human flesh.

Black Hood fell back from the door, staggered by his first contact with that hissing gray hell. He threw back his head, looked above at steam pipes that crisscrossed overhead. And then Burkey manipulated the valve that controled the overhead pipes, and the steam poured down upon Black Hood from above.

He couldn't see now, because of the steam. He dared not open his eyes lest the heat blind him permanently. But in that brief glimpse upward, Black Hood had marked the location of one of the steam pipes. He crouched, nerves and muscles tense, controled in spite of the torturous cloud of scalding vapor that pressed close to him. Suddenly, he unleashed all the pent-up power of flexed legs, leaped into the air, one gauntlet protected hand outthrust for the pipe which he knew was there even if he could not see it. Fingers grasped, held like steel hooks. He drew himself up with one powerful arm until his other hand could join its mate.

The intense heat penetrated the leather palms of his black gauntlets. Still he hung on, drawing himself upward to hook a leg over the very pipe that threatened to boil him alive. He understood now why the Hermit, that wise old man who had nursed him from the very jaws of death, had been so insistent upon regular muscular exercise. The power to save himself was there in the muscles of back, legs and arms. It was there, waiting for just such moments of danger as these.

Gradually, he hauled himself to the pipe above, got his feet onto the pipe and stood erect, his hands reaching up to the rafters to maintain his balance. And there he waited in that hot gray cloud that pressed to the roof where it condensed and fell like warm rain. His body was safe from direct contact with the blistering jets of steam.

At last the steam was shut off, the gray clouds dissipated. Cautiously, Burkey unlocked the door which connected the car washing room with his office. He stepped out, doubtless expecting to find Black Hood curled up on the floor, all consciousness driven from him by the pain of countless steam burns. The Black Hood, watching from the pipes above, showed white teeth in a wide grin.

"Look up, Burkey!" he sang out.

And as the big service station proprietor raised startled eyes, the Black Hood let go of the rafters, took a dive from the pipe straight at the man below. He caught Burkey at the throat and shoulders with his hands. The driving weight of him crushed the big man to the floor, knocked the breath out of him. And for a moment Black Hood just sat there on top of Burkey, holding him in his powerful grasp.

"How does it feel to be utterly helpless, Burkey?" he said quietly. "You see what I can do with you? I can choke the life out of you this way." The fingers of his right hand constricted on Burkey's throat until the man's eyes crawled a little way out of their sockets. Then he leased his grip a little.

"Or I could dash your brains out against the floor like this."

And Black Hood seized Burkey's shaggy hair and bounced the filling station operator's head against the floor a couple of times.

BURKEY said nothing. Black Hood slapped him hard across the side of the face with his gauntlet covered hand. Burkey winced, squirmed a little. Then realizing that he was completely at the Black Hood's mercy, he lay still.

"Talk!" Black Hood said. "Who is the Eye?"

"I don't know," Burkey croaked. "I've never seen him. I don't know who he is. You could kill me maybe, but you couldn't make me talk."

"What was that telephone number you just called?" Black Hood persisted.

Burkey's eyes rolled. "I can't tell you. The Eye would kill me if I told."

Black Hood laughed harshly. "And what do you think I'm going to do if you don't talk?"

Burkey said nothing.

Black Hood got off the man, stood up. He told Burkey to get to his feet.

"And you'd better get your fists up, Burkey, because if you don't I'm liable to knock your head off."

Possibly Burkey knew something about boxing. Possibly he had gone a round or two with some second rate slugger some time in his life. But certainly he had never fought with anybody who could equal the Black Hood in speed and fire power. Black Hood's fists were everywhere at once. His long arms were like rapiers, striking through Burkey's guard to land time after time in the big man's face.

Finally, Burkey crumpled against the wall, one eye closed, the other looking sleepy. Blood was dripping from nose and mouth.

"Talk!" Black Hood demanded, one closed fist raised like a hammer above the man's head.

Burkey simply shook his head feebly and collapsed, unconscious.

Black Hood made a swift but careful search of the filling station office without revealing anything in the way of incriminating evidence. If Burkey knew the Eye's telephone number he apparently kept it in his head.

Black Hood found a short length of chain and a padlock which was used to keep anyone from tampering with one of the oil pumps that topped a steel drum. He returned to the car washing room, scooped the keys out of the unconscious Burkey's pockets. Then he chained and locked the filling station man to the steel cross member of the wash rack. Then he went into the office, telephoned police headquarters. When the desk sergeant had answered, he said:

"If you will send men to the Super-Charged Gas station here in your city, you will find the proprietor, a man named Burkey. I suggest that he be questioned in conjunction with the activities of the criminal organizer known as the Eye, and especially in his connection with the killing and robbery at the Weedham Industries plant tonight."

"Who is this?" the desk sergeant demanded.

Black Hood chuckled. "You'll never find out!" And then he hung up, left the station to vanish into the murk of the rain swept night.

It must have been at about this time that Joe Strong, that demon photographer on the staff of Jeff Weedham's paper, *The Daily Opinion*, made a startling discovery. He was in the dark room at the newspaper office with Barbara Sutton, developing films which he had exposed at the Weedham factory that night.

He turned from his developing traps to face Barbara. The broad grin on his coarse features was illuminated by the ruby light hanging above their heads.

"Honey," Joe said, "I got something that's going to set little old New York right back on its heels. I've got positive proof that will identify the dirty bum who's behind this crime wave. Positive evidence that will point to the killer of that watchman at the Weedham plant tonight."

There was a skeptical gleam in Barbara's beautiful eyes. Since she had been working on the newspaper with Joe Strong assigned as her pix man, she had heard just such claims from Joe before. He was always turning up a picture that was to be the scoop of the week and which usually developed into a fogged film of no use to anybody.

She said, "Well, if you have you'd better turn it over to the editor before you bungle the developing some way. Jeff Weedham is going to have to pull something pretty soon to pick up circulation. He's got to prove to his father that he can run this business. If he fails at this job as he has at every other, I understand Mr. Weedham is going to cut Jeff off from the Weedham fortune."

Joe stuck his thumbs in the arm holes of his vest.

"Jeff's worries are over, permanently. This is the scoop of the week. We got the guy red handed. Take a look, beautiful."

Joe held up the negative strip which he had just developed. He pointed a thick forefinger at the exposure near the end of the strip. Joe didn't quite understand how he had got the picture unless that flare of lightning had acted as a flashlight bulb and the lens of his camera had been open at the time. But no matter how he had obtained it, there was the picture.

It showed the unmistakable figure of Black Hood standing over Joseph, the Weedham gate keeper. It showed more than that. It showed Black Hood's gauntlet covered right hand grasping the knife that was plunged into Joseph's throat.

Barbara raised her hand to her mouth to check a startled cry. She stared at the negative and repeatedly shook her head.

"I don't believe it," she whispered. "He wouldn't do such a thing. It's a trick, Joe. You're trying to trick me."

"Not me," Joe said. "Just because you're in love with Black Hood you're trying to kid yourself. I always said that guy was a crook. And now there's proof. He's the Eye. He's the brains behind all this robbery and murder that resulted in looted banks and jewelry stores. The camera don't lie, Babs. And this little picture catches Mr. Hood with the goods on him."

Barbara's indrawn breath sounded like a sob. She turned quickly and ran from the dark room. Was it true? Could it possibly be true? Black Hood had always told her that he was an outlaw, and she had loved him in spite of that because of the many good and brave things he had done to defend people against the criminals of the underworld.

But if Black Hood *was* guiltless—this had never occurred to Barbara before—if he was actually guiltless, why had he never let her see his face?

CHAPTER V

The Brand Of Light

BUT Barbara Sutton *had* seen the face of the Black Hood. She saw it on the following night when a group of wealthy and influential citizens met at Gracelawn, the West End Avenue estate of William Weedham. Barbara saw Black Hood's face without knowing it, for in the identity of Kip Burland he had been with her all evening.

It was a pleasant face, sun-bronzed and well-formed, with waving brown hair and eyes that could be gentle and compassionate. Kip Burland had taken Barbara to dinner, much to the annoyance of Joe Strong, and later in the evening they had picked up Joe and driven in Barbara's car to the Weedham home.

Barbara was obviously deeply concerned over the evidence which Joe Strong had accidently turned up. The picture of Black Hood in the apparent act of thrusting a knife into the throat of the Weedham Industries watchman, had been plastered all over the front page of Jeff Weedham's *Daily Opinion*. Other newspapers had taken up the cry, demanding that the Black Hood be taken dead or alive.

When Barbara mentioned this news story to Kip Burland, Kip scarcely knew what was the wisest course to pursue. If he defended the Black Hood he ran the risk of exciting suspicion. The secret that Kip Burland and the Black Hood were one and the same persons was more precious than ever, now that Black Hood was wanted for murder.

"There's just one thing, Babs," he told the girl as they drove to the Weedham home, "nobody can tell me that Black Hood and this criminal genius known as the Eye are the same. I can't believe it."

"Listen, Burland," Joe Strong put in angrily, "you're not sitting there and calling me a liar, either. All these stick-up jobs recently have been planned by the Eye. You'll agree to that, no doubt. That one last night at the Weedham works was the same sort of a thing—every possible witness murdered. And I not only saw the Black Hood with my own eyes, but I took a picture of him. And then he and I had a little scrap."

"How does it happen the Black Hood isn't right down in Tombs prison now?" Kip Burland asked mildly.

"Well, er," Joe stammered, "some of his men pitched in on me from behind. There must have been three of them, anyway."

Burland could scarcely repress a laugh.

"Only three? Why, you're slipping, aren't you, Joe?"

The bickering might have gone on the rest of the evening except that Barbara Sutton told them they were both being very foolish. If Kip didn't stop his arguing, she wouldn't vouch for him at this meeting tonight at the Weedham home. She and Joe were to cover the meeting for *The Daily Opinion,* but she had simply brought Kip along as a friend, trusting that that would be enough to get him in.

Barbara Sutton's name was a prominent one in social circles as was that of Joe Strong, so that there was no difficulty gaining admittance into the Weedham home for Kip Burland. In the magnificent reception hall, Kip was introduced to Jeff Weedham. The lanky heir to the Weedham wealth was cordial.

"D-d-don't see why you want to sit in on a stuffy meeting like this just for pleasure," Jeff Weedham said, smiling, "but I can assure you that any friend of Barbara's is a friend of mine."

THE tall oak door of the library was opened by William Weedham himself—a plump, white-haired man with black, overhanging eyebrows.

"Son," he said to Jeff, "we're all ready to begin. As the owner of a newspaper which is instrumental in molding public opinion, you ought to welcome this opportunity to serve your community."

Jeff Weedham laughed. "Since the Eye or the Black Hood, whatever his name is, swiped my roadster, d-d-don't you think I'm not interested in laying him by the heels, D-d-dad."

William Weedham brought scowling eyes to focus upon Kip Burland.

"I don't believe I know this young man," he said.

Jeff said, "This is Kip Burland, a friend of mine, D-d-dad. He wants a try-out as a reporter. And I thought I'd let him help cover this business together with Joe and Barbara."

And that fixed it up. With a whispered warning to Kip to try and look like a would-be reporter, Jeff Weedham led Burland into the library. The elder Weedham took his place at the head of a long refectory table about which were seated six men. Some of those included in the committee which had been formed to take protective measures against the master criminal known as the Eye, were familiar to Kip Burland. There was short, beefy Sergeant McGinty, a representative from the police who was to serve as coordinator. McGinty, Kip Burland knew well enough, was the most ardent enemy of the Black Hood on the police force.

Then there was a cocky little man with sandy hair and one glass eye. He was Major Paxton, a retired army man and brother-in-law of William Weedham. Paxton made his home at the Weedham estate and quite naturally had been included in the group.

The tall, grim man with the long side whiskers was Harold Adler, an executive of the Bankers Express service. Certainly he had a grievance against the Eye after that attack on his guards and armored truck at the Weedham plant on the night before.

Kip Burland also recognized the handsome, energetic man with the sleek black hair and small, waxed mustache. This was Jack Carlson who operated the Atlas Auto Livery and some sort of a trucking concern. Just exactly why Carlson should have been called into this group, Kip did not know. He knew something of Carlson's past, perhaps more than even Sergeant McGinty did, and there were some blotches of shadow on Mr. Carlson's life story.

William Weedham rapped the meeting to order, remarked briefly that they had come here tonight to see if some definite plan could not be formed to cope with the ever rising danger of a major crime wave, planned and directed by this man who called himself the Eye.

"We are fortunate," the elder Weedham said, "in having Mr. Carlson with us tonight. It has been frequently said by the police that if taxi companies and other common carriers would cooperate with the law more closely, there would be much less chance for the criminal to escape. Mr. Carlson has a message for us which I hope will be representative of all members of all taxi and transport systems."

"It seems to me," Major Paxton put in, his small body swelling with importance, "that the crux of the whole matter lies in the fact that these criminals, who are operating under the direction of the Eye, have discovered some fool proof means of escaping from the scene of their crime. Is that correct, Sergeant McGinty?"

McGinty's face reddened. "I don't know whether you'd call it the crux or not, Major, but in any crime if a criminal has some fool proof means of escape, as you put it, there isn't a whole lot the police can do about it."

Somebody snickered. It was obvious that Major Paxton's remark hadn't been a particularly bright one.

"But I'll say this," the sergeant went on, "this fellow the Eye, and I prefer to call him the Black Hood, has developed a means of moving criminals beyond our reach to a hell of a high point." The sergeant coughed and apologized for his bit of profanity. "I mean, he's got a hole in the police dragnet big enough so you could drive a whole mechanized division of the army through it. If Jack Carlson can throw any light on the matter, I'd like to hear him do it."

JACK Carlson stood up, smiled smoothly, and bobbed his head to Sergeant McGinty.

"I think, gentlemen," he began, "that you will find few taxi operators in the city of New York who would not gladly assist in halting an escaping criminal if they were given the opportunity. And the same goes for any other common carrier—the railroads, bus service, and airlines. At the same time, common carriers are obliged by law not to discriminate against a prospective passenger just because he may look suspicious: That is, if I am driving a cab and a man rushes out of a bank with what I may interpret as a look of guilt upon his face, I cannot refuse to take him as a fare. Nor can I very well ask for his finger prints and check up to see if he has a criminal record before taking him to his destination."

"We know all that, Carlson," Harold Adler said. "Suppose you tell these men what you told me before the meeting."

Carlson frowned, remained dramatically silent for a moment while he twisted his mustache. Kip Burland watched the man closely. If this was acting, Carlson was a remarkable actor. Somehow, he could not trust the man nor the words that came from his mouth.

Carlson said, "The Eye has not only organized the various mobs of gunmen in this city, but he has accomplished something else. He has established a perfect underground railway for transporting these criminals from one place to another in secret. I know, because the Eye personally asked me to handle that part of his business for him."

There was another dramatic pause. Then Sergeant McGinty sprang to his feet.

"Say, Mr. Carlson, if the Eye approached you personally let's have it right now. Is the Eye this same guy known as the Black Hood?"

Carlson smiled. "It would seem so from the picture which appeared this morning in the Daily Opinion."

"Yeah," Joe Strong put in. "That's the picture I took."

No one was paying any attention to Joe. All eyes were focused upon Jack Carlson.

"Understand," Carlson continued, "I did not meet the Eye face to face. He called me on the telephone, spoke to me in a whispering voice. He asked me if I would be interested in a money-making proposition.

I played him along, tried to draw him out. He wanted me to employ cars and trucks for the secret transportation of criminals and in exchange I was to get a cut of the money which would be looted by his criminals."

"And," Weedham said, "you believe that some transportation company in this city is actually assisting the Eye in this business?"

"Undoubtedly," Carlson said. "I, of course, rejected his offer. I was attempting to figure out a plan by which I might trace this call to the Eye's hideout, but that's quite difficult with these dial phones, you know.

"But that is how the Eye is working his get-aways. He probably has carefully placed stations all over the city where criminals who are fleeing from some crime can get a fast car, or hide in some unsuspicious looking truck to be transported beyond the reach of the law. It would appear to me—"

Every light in the big room suddenly went out. Smothering blackness dropped like a shroud over those at the refectory table and upon Barbara Sutton, Joe Strong, Kip Burland, and Jeff Weedham who were seated along one wall.

"D-d-damn!" Jeff Weedham stuttered. "What's this—the well known blackout?"

A white beam of light stabbed through the French windows at the end of the room, spotted the wall directly above Jack Carlson's sleek head. In the center of the spot was a crude sign, projected in black lines upon the wall. It was like a child's drawing of a human eye, round, staring, and at the same time infinitely menacing.

Kip Burland was on his feet while the others remained spellbound by the brand of light. Watching the projected sign of the eye upon the wall, he nevertheless moved swiftly and silently toward the French windows.

The sign of the Eye flicked out, and in its place was a message in black letters:

CARLSON HAS DEFIED ME.
HE WILL DIE.

Burland waited for no more, but slipped through the French windows and onto the terrace. The white beam of light rayed out from a thick grove of shrubs and small trees on the other side of the big yard. Kip Burland raced across the lawn toward the source of the light.

CHAPTER VI

The Lady In White

HALF way toward the thicket, Kip Burland saw that the light had gone out. But he had marked the spot from which it had originated, and in another moment he had broken through the tangled branches of the shrubs to the place from which the light ray had come. He saw no one. He stopped, listening. On his left he heard the crackling of twigs. He moved quickly in that direction, saw now a wraithlike figure in white.

"Hello there."

It was the soft voice of a woman who called. Kip Burland took a few more cautious steps in the direction of the figure in white. Now that his eyes were more used to the gloom, he could see that the woman was not alone. There was a man standing beside her.

"Hello," Kip responded calmly. He took a box of matches from his pocket, struck one, and held it high. The woman wore a white evening gown. Her beautifully molded face was nearly as white as her dress. Her hair was black as India ink, drawn back from her rounded forehead to knot softly at the back of her head. Her eyes were cool green with an exotic lift at the outer extremities of the lids.

The man beside her was evidently her chauffeur, judging from his uniform. He was a dark, somber looking man with a particularly ugly scar on his chin.

The woman smiled—a smile that did not quite reach her green eyes.

"Are you the man with the flashlight who was out here a moment ago?" she asked.

Kip's eyes narrowed. He wondered if the woman was beating him to the draw. He might have asked her, and with better reason, if it was she who had turned that beam of light on the Weedham house.

The match burned out in Kip's fingers. He tossed the stub of it aside.

"Obviously I'm not the man with the flashlight," he said evenly, "or I would not have had to light a match just now."

"How silly of me," the woman with the green eyes laughed. "Of course you are not. But I am so anxious to find my little locket. I am Vida Gervais, and I live just over the wall in the next house. I think I lost my little locket while walking here this afternoon. I hoped that you were the man with the flashlight and could help me find it."

"Don't you find that gown something of a liability hunting in this jungle?" Kip asked. Her explanation was entirely too glib to suit him.

But before she could form an answer, the whip-crack of a shot rang out from the direction of the Weedham house. The woman who had introduced herself as Vida Gervais uttered a short, sharp cry. Then she and her chauffeur turned and fled.

Kip Burland thrashed his way through the bushes to the border of the thicket. In the dim night glow, he saw a man running toward the house and a second figure that lay huddled on the lawn in front of the terrace steps. Burland could not be absolutely certain, but he thought that the running man was Jack Carlson. There were hoarse shouts from the immediate vicinity of the house, and Kip recognized the bellow of Joe Strong and the harsh rasping voice of Sergeant McGinty.

Kip broke away from the shrubbery and ran across the open lawn toward that point where the man lay on the ground. The second figure, which he thought was Jack Carlson, was now kneeling beside the fallen man.

In another moment, Kip saw that his first impression had been correct. The second man was Carlson. He looked up at Kip, his face chalk white in the uncertain light.

"He's dead," Carlson said. "He's been shot."

Burland dropped beside Jack Carlson, brought out his matches, struck one. The man on the ground was wearing an ordinary business suit. He was entirely bald, with a large, shapeless nose and chubby cheeks. He was lying on one side, his left arm extended. Clutched in the dead fingers of his left hand was a yellow slip of paper. It looked like bank check paper to Burland.

Others were coming from around the side of the house—Jeff Weedham and Barbara Sutton. Behind them came Major Paxton and two other members of the committee.

KIP Burland shot a glance at Jack Carlson, saw that the latter was looking in the direction of the newcomers. Kip thrust out a hand toward the piece of yellow paper in the fingers of the corpse. It was so rapid a movement that even if Carl-

son had been watching him it is doubtful if the auto livery operator could have caught it. Kip jerked the piece of paper from the hand of the dead man, and stood up.

By the time Barbara and Jeff Weedham had joined them, Burland had rolled the slip of yellow paper into a cylinder and placed it inside the cap of his fountain pen.

"Kip!" Barbara gasped. "What's happened?"

"Someone seems to have been shot," he replied mildly. "I don't know just who."

Jeff Weedham had a flashlight. He turned the beam on the face of the dead man.

"D-d-damn!" he stammered. "It's Biggert. Poor old Biggert. Why, he's D-d-dad's private secretary. Attended to everything for D-d-dad."

William Weedham, Adler, and the rest of the committee men hurried from the corner of the house.

"Biggert, did you say?" William Weedham gasped. "Good lord! Where's that Sergeant McGinty?" And then Weedham dropped beside the dead man, looked long and searchingly into the immobile face.

Sergeant McGinty put in his appearance a moment later and with him was Joe Strong. He was holding onto Joe by the ear.

"Try your football tackles on me, will you!" McGinty was growling, while Joe was trying to break away without losing an ear.

"Aw, Sergeant, how did I know it was you prowling around in all that dark?" Joe complained.

It was evident that Joe had made another of his unfortunate mistakes. But McGinty forgot and forgave when he saw the body of Biggert lying there on the lawn. The sergeant bent his thick knees, took Jeff Weedham's flashlight, turned it on the corpse.

"It was obviously a mistake," Jack Carlson was explaining smoothly. "The killer had no designs on Biggert, certainly."

"Huh?" McGinty looked up, his red face contorted by a puzzled frown. "What do you mean, it was a mistake?"

"This is obviously the Eye's work," Carlson explained. "I was standing just about in this spot when this man Biggert came running around the house and directly in front of me. That was when the shot was fired. The bullet was intended for me. You would expect as much after the Eye's warning."

McGinty nodded his head. "Could be. And believe me, Mr. Carlson, you'd better put yourself under police protection."

"I can take care of myself, thanks," Carlson insisted. As he turned away from McGinty and the body, his eyes met those of Kip Burland. And then Carlson stepped quickly to the outer rim of the circle around the body.

Kip Burland knew that Carlson was lying. Carlson hadn't been near Biggert at the time of the shooting. It was Carlson whom Burland had seen running toward the body.

"D-d-dad," Jeff Weedham stammered, "where was Biggert when we were in the library?"

"Oh, how should I know!" The elder Weedham ran his fingers through his gray hair. "I don't know where he was. In his room, I suppose, going over my personal accounts."

"Possibly," Major Paxton put in, "he was disturbed when the lights went out in the house and came down to investigate. He probably heard the rest of us outside the house, searching for that prowler who turned the light through the library window."

"And possibly," McGinty said, "Biggert had discovered something pretty important, too! There's a little scrap of yellow paper in his fingers—just a corner, as though somebody snatched a note or something from his hand."

"Just a corner, you say, Sergeant?" Jack Carlson asked. "When he fell in front of me, I noticed that there was quite a sizable slip of paper in his hand."

"There was, huh?" McGinty's eyes rested accusingly upon each face in the circle about the body. "All right. Now just tell me who first joined you and the murdered man, Mr. Carlson."

Carlson looked at Kip Burland. "It was that young man," he said.

"Burland, huh?" McGinty said. "I guess I'll have to search your pockets, Burland, if you've no objection."

Kip smiled. "None whatever, Sergeant."

McGinty went through Kip's pockets. He ignored the fountain pen which was clipped in plain sight. He stood back, shook his head.

"I guess you're clean, Burland," he admitted, and then turned to the others. "But

I'm finding whatever was in Biggert's hand, understand? Mr. Weedham, you'll go call headquarters and tell them I want the Homicide Detail out here."

"You mean me, d-d-don't you?" Jeff Weedham asked.

McGinty shook his head. "I mean your father. You and the rest stay here. I'll have a little more searching to do. And a lot more questions to ask."

Though McGinty fulfilled his promise in so far as the questions and the searching were concerned, he didn't turn up the piece of paper he was looking for. Neither did he find the weapon or the murderer.

It was about eleven o'clock when Jack Carlson asked permission to leave. He had some urgent business to attend to, he explained to the sergeant. McGinty had no grounds for holding Carlson, told him to go ahead.

But Carlson did not leave alone. Kip Burland, without asking permission from anybody or even saying good-night to Barbara, slipped quietly from the house. He was particularly interested in the urgent business which was pressing Mr. Jack Carlson.

CHAPTER VII

The Trail Of The Beam

IF JACK Carlson was as innocent as he pretended to be, it was curious that he should stop just outside the gate of the Weedham home, reach into a bed of dwarf evergreens from which he took a long copper cylinder which closely resembled a flashlight.

From his hiding place in the shadows, Kip Burland saw this move on the part of Carlson. He then saw Carlson get into his car and drive away. Burland hailed a passing cab, ordered the driver to keep Carlson's car in sight.

Carlson drove down into the lower east side of town, parked his car in a narrow street, and got out. Kip ordered his cab to pass Carlson's car. Looking back through the rear window, he saw Carlson turn up a narrow walk between two tenement buildings.

"Stop here," Kip ordered the cab driver. And as the taxi braked, he got out, threw a bill to the driver, and ran up the street toward the place where Carlson had disappeared.

In the dusky shadows between the two tenements, Burland watched Carlson put something into a wooden milk box attached just outside what was apparently someone's ktichen door. Then Kip had to duck back into a darkened doorway as Carlson retraced his steps, and got back into his car.

Kip had to make a choice quickly. Either he continued to follow Carlson or he investigated the milk box which Carlson had mysteriously visited. In as much as there was no taxi in sight, Kip decided on the latter course. As soon as Carlson was out of sight, he left the doorway, went up the walk between the two buildings, opened the milk box.

Inside the box he found the copper cylinder which he had seen Carlson take from its hiding place outside the Weedham home. The thing resembled a flashlight more closely than ever on close inspection. It was a little longer than the usual three cell case, and there was a finely ground lens at the end.

Around the outside of the case was a piece of paper, held in place by a rubber band. Kip removed the rubber band, unrolled the paper, studied it in match light. On the paper was penciled the name "Delancy" followed by the words, "Second floor rear at end of fire escape, sixty-eight A Seventh Avenue." At the bottom of the paper was that crude drawing, the sign of the Eye.

Kip's pulse quickened. Could it be that Carlson was the Eye? Certain here was a message which Carlson had delivered and which carried the Eye's signature. And the flashlight device—Kip understood its construction and purpose immediately. Inside the case was some sort of a trigger mechanism operated by a button on the outside. The trigger operated a narrow strip of film, perhaps eight millimeter film, on which were photographed the messages which the Eye intended to send. This film would be placed between the light globe and the lens, so that the photographed message could be projected on any wall from a long distance.

This was the device which had been used tonight at the Weedham home. Someone on the outside, probably the lady with the green eyes, Vida Gervais, had employed the light beam projected message. That warning which seemed to have been intended for Carlson was probably no warning at all. Perhaps the police had been keeping rather a sharp eye on Carlson, and Carlson had decided to put himself in the clear by faking that little scene at the Weedham's and pretending that the Eye intended to kill Carlson.

"And that would be suicide, I'd be willing to bet my last dollar!" Kip muttered grimly.

He replaced the light signal device in the milk box together with the note which was attached to the copper case. He would await further developments. Carlson was the Eye, he was certain. It was now the job of the Black Hood to catch Carlson red-handed.

HE left the narrow corridor between buildings to take up a post on the other side of the street. He did not have to wait very long until a man in the garb of a telegraph messenger came up the street. The messenger looked both ways and finally turned up that sidewalk between the two tenements. Even from where he stood, Kip Burland could hear the rattle of the milk box top. A moment later, the messenger appeared. He was carrying that self-same copper cased flashlight device.

It was a tangled trail that Kip Burland followed that night, shadowing that man who wore a telegraph messenger's costume. From half a block behind the man, Kip watched the messenger walk along side of the bleak walls of Tombs prison. He saw the narrow ray of that signal beam reach out and up to one of the narrow, barred windows. The Eye was signaling to someone who was even now in the hands of the police!

The further he delved into the mystery of the whispering criminal known as the Eye, the more intriguing it became. Who but a perverted genius could have planned so completely, so thoroughly that not even prison walls offered any sort of a barrier?

It was when the messenger crossed over to Seventh Avenue that Kip Burland decided that this time he would be on the receiving end of that message that traveled the light beam. He knew where the messenger was heading. That paper banded to the flashlight device had carried a Seventh Avenue address. Someone else was to receive one of the Eye's little missives. A man by the name of Delancy, judging from the writing on the note paper.

The name struck a responsive cord in Kip Burland's memory. It recalled Ray

Delancy, one of the most dangerous rob and kill men in the business. Delancy would be the sort of a person valuable to the Eye.

IN a murky alley off Seventh Avenue, Kip Burland paused for a few precious moments. Quickly, he shed his outer garments, revealing beneath the yellow silk tights, the wide belt, and the black athletic shorts that identified the Black Hood. From the inter-lining in the back of his suit coat, he took a flat folded package composed of his gauntlet gloves, his black silk cape, and that combination mask and hood that completed the costume. Shortly, Kip Burland had vanished, completely overshadowed by his famous alias—the Black Hood.

The Eye's messenger had been moving at a leisurely pace. In spite of the delay his costume change had necessitated, Black Hood easily outstripped the messenger, reached the Seventh Avenue address which had been noted on that slip of paper attached to the signal device. This proved to be an ancient red brick lodging house which would have made an excellent hideout for a criminal.

There was a fire escape on the side of the building. Black Hood raised his eyes to the second story, marked the window which was nearest the fire escape at this point. This was the window mentioned in the Eye's instructions. Just across the alley from this point, Black Hood spied a wood telephone pole. He grinned. Nothing could be sweeter! He crossed to the pole, leaped for the lowest climbing spike, driven into the wood about eight feet from the ground, and drew himself upwards. At the second climbing spike, he stopped. From this position he would be able to see the upper part of the wall of the second floor room of the building across the alley, and also the ceiling. He pulled his black cape around him and waited.

It wasn't long before he heard the footsteps of the messenger crunching along the alley. The man came to a stop within a few feet of the very post to which Black Hood was clinging. He pointed the copper cased flashlight device upward toward the dark window which Black Hood was watching. The white ray stabbed out through the darkness, and Black Hood could clearly see the brand of the Eye, projected on the ceiling of the room across the alley.

The light beam lingered for a moment, then went out. The shadowy figure of a man appeared at the window. A cigarette glowed in his lips. A signal, Black Hood wondered? And then the figure in the window withdrew and the light beam again shot up from below. This time the words of the Eye's message were clearly projected onto the ceiling of the crimester's hideout. Black Hood read:

"Delancy, come to headquarters at once." And then the beam of light went out.

Black Hood altered his position slightly so that he clung to the pole with one hand, his body poised for a leap. The faint rustle of the Black Hood's cape caused the messenger on the ground to look up.

Black Hood knew that he had to act fast. That signaling device which the messenger carried was an important piece of evidence. Jack Carlson's finger prints would be on the case. That, together with the photo film which carried the Eye's message and was enclosed in the trigger mechanism of the novel projector, constituted evidence that would prove that Jack Carlson was the Eye.

Black Hood sprang out from the pole, swooped down upon the messenger like a huge black bat. The man turned to flee too late. Black Hood caught him by the coat tails, dragged him back. The messenger turned, grappled with Black Hood. Then followed one of those grim, silent struggles, too deadly serious for oaths and threats. Rat this pawn of the Eye may have been, but even a cornered rat will fight with the courage of a lion.

Time after time the man tried to bash Black Hood's skull with the copper cased signal device—tried once too often; for Black Hood's gauntlet covered fingers closed like steel hooks upon the device. A twist, a sudden jerk, and it was Black Hood who had the signal device now.

The copper cylinder gone, the messenger's courage seemed to have gone with it. He turned, fled like a frightened rabbit up the alley and into the avenue.

Again Black Hood was faced with one of two choices. He might follow the messenger, might catch him, turn him over to the cops. But in all probability, the messenger knew less about the identity of the Eye than Black Hood knew. He was merely a tool in the hands of a master criminal. And Black Hood was after that master criminal.

The second choice, and the one which

he decided to take, was to follow Delancy who had been given orders from the Eye to appear at the headquarters of the mob immediately. And in as much as Black Hood had not the slightest idea where the Eye had his headquarters, this was the wisest course to pursue.

His heart beat high with hope as he waited in the alley for Delancy to make his appearance. He felt that he was nearing the end of the case, approaching the time when the Eye, that menace to the peace and safety of all New York, could be placed behind prison bars. And when he had proved that Jack Carlson was the Eye, Black Hood would clear himself of the charge of murder!

CHAPTER VIII

The Forces Of Evil

THE Eye had chosen his headquarters well. It was in the basement room of what had once been a Greenwich Village speakeasy. There he had brought together all of the important rival mobs of the city—forces of evil which might otherwise have been at each other's throats. The Eye had brought unity to the underworld. He had taught them that there was nothing to be gained by warring among themselves; and there were millions to be gained by united action.

Delancy was there, his toadlike form crouching on the edge of his chair placed next to that of Ron "The Bug" Brayton, formerly Delancy's rival in the rob and kill profession. All of Delancy's star gunsels were there—Squid Murphy, Shiv and the rest.

The Eye was there, standing on a rough wood platform at one end of the room. His coat was off so that anyone present might plainly see the twin gun harness he wore and the black butts of two heavy automatics. His face and head was covered with a full mask of thin white rubber, pierced by two slots for eyeholes. He wore a black slouch hat.

Black Hood was there, but nobody knew about that except the guard at the top of the basement stairway. The guard knew, but bound and gagged he was in no position to say anything about it. Black Hood stood in that shadowy stairway and was himself like one of the shadows—watching, listening, waiting for his time.

Ray Delancy shuffled to his feet as the meeting began.

"Mr. Eye," Delancy said, "I got a complaint to make, that is if you don't mind. Like to get it off my chest before we go into anything in the way of new business."

The Eye inclined his head. "Make your complaint, Mister—" He coughed. "Well, go ahead."

"It's about this man Carlson who works for you," Delancy said. "When I pulled that job at the Weedham plant for you, I was hot on the get-away. I thought I was hot, anyway. We switched paint jobs at Burkey's station, see, and rolling into town that dame you sent to ride with us switched on the radio. A police call came through. The coppers were looking for us. I didn't figure how come until a good bit later."

"Go on," the Eye said.

Delancy shuffled his feet and looked at the floor.

"I don't like to make trouble, see, but that was a put-up job."

"You mean what?" the Eye questioned.

"I mean that wasn't no police call. There was some sort of a phonograph device under the cowl of that get-away car, and this was hooked up to the radio switch. That police call was a phoney. We wasn't hot. That was just rigged up to send us to Jack Carlson to ask that he get us out of town in a hurry.

"I went to Carlson. I told him we was hot, because at the time I figured we was. He wanted fifty per cent of our total take to move us out of town. Fifty per cent, and with the ten that we are supposed to pay you, that don't leave a guy much profit. I told Carlson I'd rot in jail first. And all the time, I ain't hot at all, because the bulls haven't turned the heat on me. It was a phoney, see, just to get me to spend a lot of dough on a get-away."

The Eye nodded. "There have been some other complaints about Carlson. I will see that he is eliminated. Someone else will take over the position which he has filled."

In the shadows of the stairway, Black Hood laughed soundlessly. That was a hot one, that was! Here was Carlson, playing both ends against the middle, getting his cut as the Eye and getting a second and large helping out of his crooked transport business. And now the Eye was talking about eliminating Carlson to appease Ray Delancy!

"To get back to the business at hand," the Eye said, "our next job is a small matter of one hundred thousand in unset jewels. And by a hundred thousand, I am not referring to the current market price. We can realize that amount from a fence. It sounds good, eh?"

Some of the mobsters cursed appreciatively.

"There is," the Eye continued, "an obscure little jewelry shop known as Tauber's which has received such a shipment of gems."

"Diamonds or other stuff?" Ron "The Bugs" Brayton asked.

The Eye coughed. "The former," he said. "Tomorrow night I will require the services of a select number of you. I'll want Murphy, and—" he nodded at Delancy— "you. You, too, Brayton, and a number of your best men. We will also need a good safe expert."

One of the crooks held up his hand. "That's me."

"Agreed, then," the Eye said. "If there is nothing else to attend to, we may as well adjourn."

AS some of the crooks started toward the foot of the steps leading up from the basement room, it appeared as though there was quite a bit more to attend to. This was the moment for which Black Hood had been waiting. Standing near the top of the stairs, he reached out and hauled the bound and helpless guard down to his level. As the first of the hoods showed his face at the foot of the stairs, Black Hood gave the guard a shove that sent the man flopping down the stairs to bowl over two of the foremost members of the mob.

The Black Hood took a couple of strides and then leaped from halfway down the steps. He cleared the roped guard and the two fallen hoods, landed lightly on the balls of his feet within a yard of Squid Murphy.

And then, before anyone in the room could quite understand what this was all about, the Black Hood unleashed a furious one-man attack on the startled crimesters. His two long arms reached out. His gloved fingers closed on Squid Murphy and the killer called Shiv simultaneously. He brought the two together, all but jerked them from their feet, to crack Murphy's head against that of Shiv. Murphy and Shiv went limp, and as they fell, Black

Hood snatched a half-drawn automatic from the shoulder holster of gunman Murphy. He stepped clear of the two men, faced the others, a mocking smile on his lips.

"I am seldom required to carry a gun, since one of my opponents nearly always gives me his," he said quietly. "It will take just one smart move from any one among you to find out whether or not the Black Hood can shoot."

Ten of the most dangerous criminals in the city plus that master-mind, the Eye, stood there in awed silence, watching that tall figure in yellow tights and black silk hood.

"I want the Eye," Black Hood said. "If you will surrender him to me, I will give the rest of you a break—a break of five minutes in which to take your chances with the law."

Black Hood knew that the criminals would make no such bargain. He was talking to stall for time. He knew that sooner or later, either he or the criminals would have to make a move. What that move would be, he had no idea. But he was ready for anything.

It was Delancy who made the first move. He had the idea that he could draw and shoot before Black Hood could discover from just what particular point of the room the danger threatened. And it was Delancy's fatal mistake. Before he had his gun out of his shoulder holster, Black Hood had fired. He had fired, remembering that cold-blooded slaughter at the Weedham Industries plant. A third black and hollow eye appeared suddenly in Delancy's forehead. The legs of the gunman bowed beneath the weight of his toadlike body. There was a dull, bewildered expression on Delancy's face as he hit the floor.

But that first shot was the spark that touched off the powder barrel. Two more followed—one that tugged at the Black Hood's cape, a second that shot out the light in the room. Black Hood backed toward the bottom of the stair. He'd plant himself there in that narrow exit, and if the crimesters thought there was an avenue of escape, let them try. The automatic in his hand bucked and barked. His only target was the flame from the snouts of the gangster guns, but agonized cries told him that at least a portion of his slugs had found their mark.

Suddenly he saw at the rear of the room,

a narrow shaft of gray light. Somebody had opened a door. For just a moment, he saw the white face of the Eye, his rubber mask glowing like the surface of a moon. Black Hood shot twice, pulled the trigger a third time only to hear the hammer click on an empty chamber.

Perhaps the Eye heard that click and understood its meaning, for it was then that he made his dash through the rear door. Black Hood knew that retreat was now his only course. He was without weapons in a battle of screaming lead. He turned, stumbled over a fallen form, caught his balance, and then took the stairway in long strides. A cop, attracted by the shooting, appeared at the top of the steps, but he was only a momentary barrier to the Black Hood— a very hard man to stop once he got under way. His fist lashed out, caught the copper on the chin. The man probably never knew exactly when the floor came up to slap the back of his lap.

Black Hood was clear of the building now, his legs working like tireless pistons. He heard the shrill scream of police sirens, and in the basement of the building the roar of gun fire still sounded. Perhaps the criminals did not know that their opponent had left. One thing was certain: Black Hood had dealt the forces of evil a hard blow that night, and he had showed the Eye that the Black Hood was hard on his trail.

Rounding a corner, Black Hood sighted a taxi cab cruising along. He dashed into the street, waving his arm. The cab stopped, the driver goggling at the strange figure that had hailed him.

"I'm in a big hurry to get to a masquerade," Black Hood said as he opened the door of the taxi.

"So that's what it is," the driver said, apparently satisfied.

As Black Hood got into the cab, he gave the address of Jack Carlson's auto livery. So the Eye thought he had escaped, did he? Black Hood chuckled. Well, he'd planned a little surprise for Jack Carlson, alias, the Eye!

CHAPTER IX

Alias, The Corpse

IT WAS after two o'clock in the morning when Black Hood alighted from the cab near the location of Jack Carlson's auto livery garage. There was not a sign of light in the garage building, and the big doors were closed and locked. Black Hood went to the side entrance. This also was locked. Reaching into one of the secret pockets of his wide black belt he removed a curiously shaped tool of finest tempered steel. He had met few locks in his adventures which this tool could not open. A deft thrust, a twist of the wrist, and the door was no longer a barrier to him.

He returned the tool to its pocket and pulled out a tiny flashlight. The ray of light seemed swallowed by the gloom of the vast, lonely room that lay before him. Here and there were parked cars, oil drums, huge vans. Black Hood wondered how many of these vehicles had been used by the members of the Eye's criminal pack.

He crossed the room to the concrete ramp that twisted up to the second story. His footsteps whispered on the ramp. On the second floor there was neither light nor sound—not so much as the squeak of a rat. His flashlight pointed out the office, partitioned off from the rest of the big room. He crossed quickly, pushed open the office door, spotted the light switch. He turned the light switch to the on position, but no illumination came from either the central fixtures nor the lamps on the desk. A queer set-up, this.

He went into Jack Carlson's private office, tried the switch in there, still without results. He pointed his flashlight beam around until it fell on the huge iron safe in the corner. The safe door was standing wide open, the interior cleanly empty. Queerer and queerer.

He paused in the center of the room, his nostrils dilated. There was a faint, pleasant odor lingering in the room—a vaguely familiar odor.

Black Hood crossed to the door of a coat closet, jerked it open. A body fell stiffly into the room, struck the carpet with a dull, jarring sound. Black Hood sprang back, turned his light down at the corpse. He dropped to his knees beside the dead man, grasped the shoulder of the coat of the corpse, turned the man over on his back. And as he saw that gray deathmask of a face, Black Hood knew that all his carefully worked out solution had tumbled like a house of cards. The corpse on the floor was that of Jack Carlson, and he had been dead for hours.

Carlson could not have been the Eye, for less than an hour ago, Black Hood had seen and fought with the Eye!

BULLETS had pierced the chest of Carlson in three places. High on the left lapel of his dark suit coat was a white smudge made by some sort of powder. Black Hood stepped to Carlson's desk, picked up an envelope and a letter opener, and returned to the body. With great care, he scraped some of the white powder from the coat lapel into the envelope. Then he moistened the flap and sealed it.

Turning the flashlight away from the body, he suddenly noticed something else. That white smudge on Carlson's coat glowed in the darkness.

The Black Hood's keen eyes narrowed on that patch of pale light. Then, as though seized by a sudden inspiration, he sprang to Carlson's desk and tipped up the desk lamp. He reached in under the shade and laid his bare hand on the lamp bulb. The glass of that bulb was warm. Then he crossed to the door, flipped the light switch to the off position, and looked back in the direction of the corpse.

The pale glow of light which came from that powder smudge on Carlson's lapel was no longer visible!

An understanding gleam came into Black Hood's eyes. At least he understood how Jack Carlson had died, even if the mystery of the identity of the Eye had deepened. He withdrew quietly from the room and left the garage.

At the fringe of dawn the next morning, Black Hood was high in the Catskills, in the mountain fastness of that whiskered old man who had been his teacher—that man known simply as the Hermit. There in the Hermit's laboratory, Black Hood and the old man made a careful analysis of that scanty sample of powder which Black Hood had scraped from the coat of the murdered Jack Carlson.

Finally, the old man straightened from the microscope over which he had been bending.

"My son," he asked of the Black Hood, "what are your findings?"

"The stuff is face powder," Black Hood said. "But it's something else, too. Mixed in with the face powder is another substance."

"Naphthionate of sodium," the Hermit said.

"That's what I thought," Black Hood nodded. "It's one of those substances which becomes phosphorescent in ultra-violet light. And those light bulbs in Jack Carlson's garage were ultra-violet bulbs. The light from them is invisible to us poor mortals. You see what that means, Hermit?"

"Not entirely," the Hermit said.

"It means that Jack Carlson was marked for murder. That face powder came from the cheek of a woman—some woman who pressed her cheek against Carlson's lapel. And a pretty gesture of affection it was, too. It made Carlson so easy to kill!

"You see, the naphthionate of sodium in that powder sticks to just about anything. Even if Carlson had brushed the face powder off, the naphthionate would still have been there. When Carlson entered the garage, he turned on the light switch. No visible light came from those bulbs—only "black light" as it is called. And the killer was waiting. In the black light, the killer could not be seen, but Carlson was perfectly targeted by that smudge of naphthionate which glowed on his lapel.

"It was all planned in advance—the lady's part to smear the powder on Carlsons' lapel, a sort of Judas kiss. And then there was the killer's part—to replace the ordinary bulbs with the ultra-violet type, and to wait with drawn gun to shoot Carlson."

"Who, then, is the Eye?" the Hermit asked.

"I'll stick to my original idea," Black Hood said after a moment's thought. "I still think that Jack Carlson is—was—the Eye. That alibi he arranged for himself at Weedham's home, that warning from the Eye which stated that Carlson was to die, his efforts to make Biggert's death look as though the killer had been shooting at Carlson instead of at Biggert—that all points to Carlson as the Eye. He was trying to make himself appear the fair-haired boy in front of Sergeant McGinty.

"Further, and I think conclusive proof, is that signal device which was used to warn' Carlson. That was Carlson's own device. It was Vida Gervais, I believe, who turned the signal light through the French windows at the Weedham house. And then later, in a previously appointed spot, she left the signal light for Carlson to pick up as he left the house.

"Carlson changed the film in that light, putting in one which would deliver two more of the Eye's messages—one of which went to Delancy, telling him to come to a meeting tonight."

Black Hood propped one foot on a laboratory stool, rested an elbow on his knee. His eyes were bright, his face animated.

"Don't you see that up to that point, Carlson was the Eye. But shortly after he had planted the signal device for his messenger to pick up, Carlson was murdered. The man who directed the criminal meeting later on wasn't Carlson, because Carlson was dead. It means that somebody took over where Carlson left off. It means that somebody muscled in on Carlson's little racket, killed Carlson, began playing the part of the Eye."

"Which means," the Hermit said, "that you're not at the end of your task yet."

"Not by a long shot," Black Hood replied. "And I'm wondering about this Vida Gervais. Is she the woman whose face powder was smeared on Jack Carlson's lapel? I thought the odor of the powder was familiar. And here's another thing I didn't mention."

Black Hood searched the pockets of his wide belt, brought out his fountain pen.

"Here's a little item which I snitched from the hand of the murdered Biggert, who was William Weedham's personal secretary. It's a check, and I've scarcely had time to look at it myself."

He unscrewed the cap of the fountain pen and removed the piece of rolled up yellow paper which he had taken from the dead Biggert's hand. He flattened out the slip of paper and placed it on the table in front of the Hermit.

It was a check in the sum of forty thousand dollars, made out to the order of Major Paxton and signed by William Weedham, the major's brother-in-law. The check had been endorsed and paid through a New York bank.

"I think this is the reason that Biggert was killed," Black Hood said. "Weedham said that Biggert was going over his personal bank account, and it's entirely possible that Biggert discovered there was something queer about that check."

"A forgery, perhaps," the Hermit suggested.

"That was my idea," Black Hood agreed. "Anyway, that gives us a couple of leads— Vida Gervais and Major Paxton. And if both of them are knocked off before I can get the truth out of them—" Black Hood laughed without mirth.

CHAPTER X

"Stop, Murderer!"

THE following morning, Kip Burland read the early edition of Jeff Weedham's paper, *The Daily Opinion*, with his breakfast coffee. The latest story concerning the criminal exploits of the Eye was headlined:

"EYE IS BLACK HOOD"—BURKEY

The following story told how A. J. Burkey, filling station operator from a northern suburb, had been held in Tombs prison for questioning in conjunction with the murder and robbery at the Weedham plant. The night before, Burkey had confessed that his boss, the criminal known as the Eye, was actually the Block Hood.

The part of the story that put a dull ache in Kip Burland's heart was the fact that it was by-lined by Barbara Sutton, *The Daily Opinion* police reporter—and more particularly the woman whom Kip Burland loved.

There was another "Eye" story, stating that the body of Jack Carlson had been found. This murder, too, was attributed to the Eye. And once again it was pointed out that the Eye and the Black Hood were one and the same.

As night fell upon the city, Kip Burland once more vanished behind the identity of the Black Hood, not without full realization that he was taking his life into his hands. Again he visited the Weedham estate on West End Avenue, this time determined to have a talk with Major Paxton.

Prowling around the house in search for a suitable entrance, Black Hood discovered that he could not have come at a worse time. William Weedham was host to Sergeant McGinty and his cops as well as a number of reporters, including Barbara Sutton and her clumsy cameraman, Joe Strong. Evidently the police expected to gain further information about the crimes of the Eye.

Black Hood took to a stout iron trellis, climbed quickly to the second story where he found a bedroom window open. He slipped into the empty bedroom and from there went into the hall. Tiptoeing down the hall, he came to a small upstairs living room in which a light burned. There, studying a European war map was Major Paxton.

Black Hood entered silently and closed

the door behind him. As the major looked up, Black Hood stepped quickly forward so that his tall figure over-shadowed that of the peppery little major.

"What—what—who—" Paxton sputtered. "Why, look here, you can't come in here like this!"

"But I am in," Black Hood said quietly. "And you won't utter a sound, or you'll force me to live up to my unjustly earned reputation as a murderer."

"But it's illegal! It—it's damnable!"

"Now sit down and cool off, Major," Black Hood said patiently. "You can blow off steam after I've left."

"Left, huh? You'll get out of here over my dead body!"

Black Hood nodded. "If necessary, even that. But first we're going to have a quiet little chat, you and I. A little talk about a check in the amount of forty thousand dollars."

"I'll not pay you one cent!" Paxton exploded. "Why, do you think you can frighten me into—"

"I have frightened you, Major," Black Hood said, smiling. "And it won't cost you a cent, either. All I want you to do is take a look at this check."

Black Hood drew the check, which he had taken from the dead fingers of the murdered Biggert, from a pocket in his belt. He held it so that Paxton could look at it. Paxton stared, and then suddenly looked at the Black Hood's eyes revealed in the slots of his black mask.

"Why, it's made out to me!"

"Remarkable, isn't it?" Black Hood said. "It was found in the fingers of the murdered Biggert." He turned the check over to show the endorsement. "Is that your signature?"

"It most certainly is! But, great heavens, I didn't receive any money from William Weedham. I'll have you know that I am a man of independent means. He's never given me a penny. Why, what does this mean?"

Black Hood studied the little man closely. He had seen liars before, and it seemed to him that if Paxton was lying he was doing a remarkable job of it.

"That's your signature, though," he persisted.

"Yes, but I didn't sign it." The major pressed a hand to his forehead. "Wait. I've an idea. A mere ghost of an idea!" He reached into his pocket and pulled out a cigarette lighter. "My signature is engraved on this lighter," he explained. "Anyone could have borrowed my lighter and traced that endorsement. Let me see the check a moment."

BLACK HOOD shook his head. "And have you destroy it?" he said with a smile. "Rather, let me see the lighter."

The major handed over the cigarette lighter. Holding it beneath the check, Black Hood could see that the signature of Paxton on the back of the check followed in every detail the engraved signature on the lighter. He handed the lighter back.

"And the signature of William Weedham," he said. "Take a look at that?"

Major Paxton scowled. He shook his head doubtfully. "It could be genuine. And then again, it could be a forgery. It seems to me—"

The door behind Black Hood opened. The master manhunter wheeled, saw the lank figure of Jeff Weedham standing in the door. Jeff Weedham opened his mouth, shouted at the top of his voice.

"D-d-dad! Help! The Black Hood!" And then young Weedham tried a necktie tackle that was supposed to flatten Black Hood to the floor.

Black Hood bent double to duck that high tackle. The result was that Jeff Weedham landed squarely across Black Hood's broad back. The manhunter straightened, threw Jeff to the floor, darted from the room and out into the hall.

The stairway was within three long strides of him. Black Hood slid half way down the broad stair railing before he saw William Weedham and Sergeant McGinty at the foot of the steps waiting for him. McGinty had his gun out. Black Hood kicked his legs over the rail, reversing his position, gave himself a shove with his hands. He dropped over the railing, landed on his feet in the hall below. He turned, dashed through a door that stood open beneath the stairs. This brought him into a huge dining room.

But he wasn't there long enough to tell about it. He went through a swinging door into a butler's pantry, then into a kitchen. There was a cop at the back door, waiting for him. He pivoted in his tracks, doubled back into the dining room, went through another door that brought him to the living room. No way out there. And then he remembered that William Weed-ham's library was between living room and hall. The French windows of the library might be the one avenue of escape which McGinty's thinly spread men were not guarding.

He reached the library, ran to the French windows. They were locked, but the key was in place. He was about to unlock the windows when he heard the door off the hall open and close.

"Stop, murderer!"

Black Hood turned, just a little slowly this time, because he had recognized that voice—a voice that haunted his dreams as did the face of the lovely girl who owned it. Barbara Sutton stood in the doorway, a small but businesslike revolver in her hand.

CHAPTER XI

The Frame Complete

"**B**ARBARA," Black Hood said quietly, "you're joking!"

She shook her head. Her lower lip trembled.

Black Hood took two steps toward her and saw her gun wrist stiffen.

"Listen," he said grimly, "I could take that penny pea shooter away from you in a second. I want you to know that I'm staying here in this room when every second of delay may spell my death. I'm staying here because if it's the last thing I do, I'm going to convince you that I'm not a killer. And I'm not the Eye."

"That picture Joe took," she said. "And that confession of the man in Tombs. And you've told me time and time again that you're an outlaw."

He nodded. "If my real identity were known, the police could take me on the charge of robbery. But that charge would be a frame, just as this one is. I can never clear myself of the robbery charge. But I can and *will* clear the Black Hood of the charge of murder. Joe must have got that picture by accident. I was simply bend-ing over that watchman at the Weedham plant gate to see if there was any chance that he was alive and had witnessed the crime. When I saw the knife, I planned to withdraw it from the watchman's throat, to use it as possible evidence.

"You've got to believe me, Barbara. I'm fighting this creature who calls himself the Eye just as you are and just as the police

are. You and I have been through a lot of adventures together. Ask yourself if I have ever done a single thing which would indicate that I would stoop to the slaugh-ter of the innocent. Ask yourself that, Bar-bara."

He took another step toward her. Her violet eyes glistened with tears.

"Joe Strong has tried to poison your mind against me," he said. "I can't blame him for that, since all's fair in love and war. But you've got to believe me, Barbara. You've got to believe me because—because I love you. I've always loved you from the first day I set eyes on you. And—"

The gun spilled from Barbara's limp fin-gers, and suddenly she was in his arms. He held her fiercely, tenderly for a long moment, kissed her warm lips. And then there were sounds of footsteps in the hall. He heard Jeff Weedham say:

"D-d-did anybody look in the library?"

Black Hood released Barbara, turned, dashed back to the French windows. He looked back before he plunged out into the darkness, and his teeth gleamed in a smile. Barbara was smiling, too—smiling and cry-ing at the same time.

There was a police guard at the gate of the Weedham estate, but then Black Hood had never cared a whole lot about using gates anyway. He raced across the lawn, vaulted over the wall which separated the Weedham property from the place belong-ing to the green-eyed Vida Gervais next door.

To all appearances, the green-eyed lady was not at home—not unless those catlike eyes of hers were capable of seeing in the dark. Black Hood found his way into the house through a window. Inside, the house was as silent as it was dark.

Eventually, he found his way to Vida Gervais' boudoir and there poked and sniffed among the boxes and jars of cos-metics on her dressing table. A box of face powder attracted his particular atten-tion, and when he looked into the adjoin-ing bathroom he discovered a suitable means of testing the powder to make sure that it was the same which he had scraped from the coat lapel of the dead Jack Carlson. Evidently, the lady was somewhat concerned about her pale complexion, for there was a sun lamp in the bathroom. Beneath its ultra-violet rays Black Hood discovered that the face powder took on a phosphorescent glow, proving that sodium naphthionate had been added to it. He took the powder with him when he left the house a few minutes later dressed in a spare uniform of Vida Gervais' chauffeur.

IT WAS an hour later that Black Hood came to an obscure little jewelry shop known simply as "Tauber's." It was here that the Eye's crimesters were supposed to pull their next job, according to the plans which had been set forth at the meeting on the night before. Whether or not Black Hood's unexpected appearance at that meeting had put a crimp in those plans, he did not know. But there was no way of learning except by trial and error. Except for a night light which glinted through the show window, the place was dark.

Black Hood reflected that had he any desire to live up to his false reputation as a criminal, he could have done very nicely for himself. It required just twenty minutes of work for him to open the window at the back of the shop—steel grill work, burglar alarm, lock and all. It was rather a tight squeeze for his broad shoulders, getting through the opening, but he managed it. No sooner had his feet hit the floor, however, than he felt the cold, stern prod of the barrel of an automatic.

"All right, Mr. Hood, put up your hands!"

Black Hood jerked a glance over his right shoulder to behold the unlovely visage of Mr. Ron "The Bugs" Brayton.

"Hi there, Bugs," he said lightly, raising his hands to the level of his shoulders. "Fancy meeting you here."

Brayton laughed. "If you'da knocked at the front door, we'd have let you in, Mr. Hood. It's pretty early for a heist, ain't it? But we figured the early bird would get the diamonds. And then you was wised up to this job, wasn't you?"

"Oh, I did hear it mentioned at the lodge meeting last night," Black Hood said. He laughed. "Isn't that Squid Murphy over there in the corner, trying to disguise himself as a corner of that safe?"

Murphy stepped out of the shadows. He had a gun in his fist. A third hood put in his appearance from the front of the store and a fourth came out of Tauber's private office.

"You're just a little bit too late, Mr. Hood," Bugs Brayton said. "That is, too late to get your hands on these beauties.'

Brayton extended his right arm in front of him. He was holding a small leather satchel, the mouth of the bag wide open. What light there was in the place scintillated on a layer of unset diamonds in the bottom of the bag. It was then that Black Hood got one of those sudden inspirations which had made him the underworld's most capable adversary. His right hand dropped with incredible swiftness to his wide black belt, snatched something from a concealed pocket there. That same hand shot out toward the bag of diamonds, lingered over its open mouth a moment before it clenched into a fist and hammered to the point of Squid Murphy's jaw.

Murphy went back very fast and didn't stop until he had rammed into the Tauber safe. But the three other hoods closed in upon Black Hood. Bugs Brayton's big automatic rose and fell like an ax. The barrel of it caught Black Hood on the temple with stunning force. Black Hood fell to the floor and an unidentified but effective shoe toe caught the side of his head with a powerful kick. Blazing blobs of light exploded within his brain, and then the total blackness of unconsciousness funneled down upon his brain.

Bugs Brayton stood over the fallen manhunter. He weighed his automatic thoughtfully in his hand. He looked at Squid Murphy and the others.

"Well, boys," he said, "I guess it's up to me to finish off Mr. Hood. And I can't say that I got any regrets about him dying so young." He laughed, stooped over Black Hood, pressed the muzzle of his gun to the manhunter's forehead.

"Stop, Bugs!" came a whispered command from the front of the store.

Brayton straightened. Coming toward the group of crimesters around the unconscious Black Hood, was the man they knew as the Eye, his white rubber mask resembling a death's head in the half light.

"It would be a grave mistake to kill Black Hood, Brayton," the Eye said. "Once he is dead, the police will turn their attention to others—perhaps to any one of us. You understand?"

"But the guy's dangerous," Squid Murphy protested. "I'll take my chances with the bulls any day, rather than with Black Hood."

"He won't be dangerous to us in prison," the criminal chief argued. "Hand me the gems, Brayton."

Brayton obeyed. He watched the Eye's

slim white fingers reach down into the layer of diamonds, watched them sift the glittering gems. Then he took a dozen or so of the stones from the bag, transferred them to a pocket in Black Hood's belt.

"Now," he said, "the frame is complete. I will take care of the gems and as soon as I have sold them, I will split with you. Let's get out of here."

So great was their fear of their leader that the crimesters obeyed without protest. Just outside the rear door of the jewelry shop, the criminal chief stopped, raised a whistle to his lips, and blew a skirling blast.

"What's the idea?" Brayton demanded, startled.

"To bring the police for the Black Hood, you fool!"

CHAPTER XII

Black Light

BLACK HOOD staggered to his feet, his brain still whirling from that blow to his head. He lurched toward the front door of the shop, stopped half way there, clung to a counter for support. Somebody was pounding on the front door. A hoarse voice was calling on him to open in the name of the law.

Black Hood turned, spurred the muscles of his legs to carry on. The brilliant light of a policeman's torch sliced through the semi-darkness and spotted him. He kept going. Glass in the front door shattered beneath a blow from the butt of the copper's revolver. Black Hood ran on leaden feet into the rear of the shop. The back door stood invitingly open. He stepped over the sill, all but fell into the arms of a second cop. He struck just one wild haymaker of a blow that cleared the head of the cop by nearly a foot. And then suddenly there were two cops—one on either side of him.

"It's Black Hood!" one of the coppers shouted triumphantly. "We've got him. We've got the Eye. Wait till Sergeant McGinty hears about this!"

Cold steel jaws of handcuffs closed on Black Hood's right wrist. A second cop frisked him quickly, emptying the pockets of his belt.

"Look at the sparklers, will you!" the policeman gasped.

And Black Hood, his mind still in a daze, stared down at the gems in the cop-per's hand. No use telling them it was a frame. That was the standard alibi of every crook who ever found his way into police courts. They had him cold, and in his present condition he was utterly unable to fight back.

As long as he lived he was never to forget that ride down to police headquarters. Nor could he ever forget standing there in Sergeant McGinty's office while the sergeant did a bit of triumphant gloating.

"As sure as my name's McGinty, I knew there'd come a day like this, Mr. Black Hood, alias the Eye. I've got you, and I've got you where I want you. You'll burn in the chair, Mr. Hood."

Black Hood stood erect, still handcuffed to the cop who had captured him. He could think a little bit more clearly now and the muscles of his powerful body were much more inclined to obey the dictates of his taut nerves. He looked at the top of the sergeant's desk. There the entire contents of his belt pockets had been spread out—the dozen diamonds which had been used to frame him; that crumpled check which he had taken from the dead fingers of Biggert; the powder box from Vida Gervais' boudoir, most of its contents now gone; all his little tools and weapons which he had found valuable in his valiant fight against crime.

"You know what I've done, Mr. Hood?" McGinty asked. "I've telephoned the members of the citizens' committee who got together to tell the police what to do to catch the Eye. I've asked them and their friends to come down here to headquarters for the unveiling of Black Hood, alias the Eye. When they get here, I'm going to jerk off that mask of yours and we'll all have a little surprise party."

"You might spare me that 'alias, the Eye' business," Black Hood said, some of his old-time banter returning. "The Eye died when Jack Carlson died, and I can prove that. Since Carlson was murdered, another has taken his place. The man who killed Biggert and also killed Jack Carlson, now wears the white rubber mask that identifies the Eye, goes around whispering orders to professional rob and kill men. He's robbed Carlson's safe and robbed Carlson of his life and even robbed Carlson of his identity as the Eye. And given half a chance, I'll prove that to you, McGinty."

McGinty frowned. He could not deny that many times before Black Hood had beaten him to the solution of crimes, much to his embarrassment. And in each case, McGinty had received full credit for the solving of these crimes.

"When the time comes, Mr. Hood," McGinty said, "you'll have your chance to speak your little piece. I wouldn't deny that to any man."

"Then perhaps you'll unlock these handcuffs," Black Hood suggested. "You've robbed my bag of all its tricks and I'm relatively harmless at the present time. Besides," he added, glancing at the cop to whom he was linked, "this man here becomes something of a liability after this length of time."

"Unlock the cuffs, Bricker," McGinty ordered the cop. "Black Hood can't get out of here, and that's a sure thing."

THE cuff removed from his right wrist, Black Hood went to a chair beside the desk and calmly sat down.

"I want to appeal to your reason a moment, Sergeant, before this committee arrives for the 'unveiling' as you call it. First of all, is it reasonable to suppose that I would crack open a jewelry store just to get those few diamonds there on the desk? And having broken into the store with intent to rob, as you seem to think, would I be silly enough to fall on my head and knock myself out?"

"Could be those were the only diamonds you found in the store."

"There were one hundred thousand dollars worth of unset diamonds in that store tonight," Black Hood said. "And that's what this man who is posing as the Eye went after and got. The past record shows that none of these crimes have been what you could call petty."

"A fact," McGinty said, "which doesn't prove you haven't hid the diamonds somewhere."

"But kept a few of them on my person just to get myself in jail, huh?" Black Hood laughed. "Listen, McGinty, why do you suppose Biggert, Weedham's secretary, was killed?"

"The shot that killed Biggert was intended for Jack Carlson," McGinty said. "So it was an accident that Biggert was shot."

Black Hood shook his head. "Jack Carlson was nowhere near Biggert when the latter fell. That was no mistake. Biggert was killed because he was about to expose

somebody who had forged that check which is lying on your desk. That check is the piece of paper that was in Biggert's hand when he died."

McGinty's eyes narrowed. "How did you get hold of that, Mr. Hood?"

Black Hood saw that he would have to lie in order to protect his prototype, Kip Burland.

"I reached the body of Biggert before Carlson or anyone else did. That's how I know Carlson wasn't near the man when the shot was fired."

McGinty thought that over a moment.

"Go ahead, Mr. Hood. I'm not convinced, but every man has a right to free speech."

"Did the police notice the smudge of white powder on the lapel of Carlson's coat when they found his body? Did they notice that the regular light bulbs in his garage had been replaced with ultra-violet bulbs?"

McGinty nodded. "Our lab men don't miss much. That smudge of powder contained some chemical that glows in black light. I figured it spotted Carlson for the killer, made a target out of him in the dark."

"Right, McGinty. But do you know that Carlson was betrayed by a woman named Vida Gervais? She lives in the house next to the Weedham place. That powder box which you took from my pocket and which is now on your desk, is a sample of her face powder, treated with naphthionate of sodium. You can prove that yourself. And if you'll question the lady thoroughly, you'll be able to get at the truth. She'll know that Carlson was the Eye. And she may even admit that she threw Carlson over and helped somebody else dispose of Carlson and step into the lucrative position which Carlson occupied as the Eye."

McGinty looked up at one of his men, "Send out for that Gervais dame." When the man had left the room, he turned to Black Hood. "You haven't cleared yourself yet. You claim Carlson was the Eye. That's the world's oldest alibi—putting the blame on a dead man."

"I can prove Carlson was the Eye," Black Hood persisted. "In the morning I will send you that signal device which the Eye used. It carries Carlson's fingerprints."

"You'll send it from jail, then," McGinty said.

BLACK HOOD shook his head. "I wonder if you'd send to the police lab for an ultra-violet lamp? I think I can conduct an experiment which will prove my points."

McGinty considered this a moment, and finally sent out for an ultra-violet lamp. It was not long after that before the members of the citizens committee began to arrive. The two Weedhams, father and son, were ushered into the room, folowed by Major Paxton, Harold Adler, and the rest of the committee. Jeff Weedham's newspaper was represented by Barbara Sutton and her ace cameraman, Joe Strong. And finally the police brought in a coldly furious Vida Gervais.

Black Hood carefully avoided meeting Barbara Sutton's eyes. He knew that her emotions must be strained to the breaking point, and even a glance from him might have caused her to betray herself.

"D-d-don't tell me you've finally caught Black Hood, Sergeant!" Jeff Weedham gasped.

The sergeant smiled. "Sooner or later, McGinty gets 'em all."

McGinty waited until all present were seated. Then he stood up alongside of Black Hood.

"Now, folks," he said, "as you can see, I've got Black Hood just where I want him. And I've wanted him quite a while. I promised you that I'd show you his face, and that's just what I'm going to do."

HAROLD ADLER uttered a hoarse cry of warning that came just a bit too late. With one of those lightning-like movements of his, Black Hood had pulled the revolver out of McGinty's holster, turned it on the sergeant. A copper near the door started to intervene, but Black Hood stopped him with a narrow-eyed glance that held all the threat of a thunderbolt.

"Make a move toward me, and I put a bullet into McGinty's back," he said. "No one will ever see the face of Black Hood and live to talk about it. I've just given McGinty the entire solution to this mystery. I've told him that Jack Carlson was the Eye. I've explained how Jack Carlson was murdered and his powerful position in the underworld was usurped by another man who now poses as the Eye. If there is any doubt in his mind, I am about to dispel it."

Black Hood picked up the ultra-violet lamp with his left hand while his right

kept the gun on McGinty. He said, "Mr. Adler, will you kindly turn out the lights."

Adler hesitated.

"Do as you're told," Black Hood insisted, "if you don't want to witness murder. And I want to warn everyone in this room, that when the lights go out if anyone makes any move toward me, McGinty will die. Even if I were to be shot, the reflex action of my fingers would pull the trigger of this revolver and McGinty will die. I am no murderer, but if you interfere with me in this business, you'll make a murderer of me."

Adler switched out the lights. The darkness lay like a smothering blanket upon them all. The air itself had a certain electrical tenseness about it, like the silence before a storm.

"I am now going to switch on the ultra-violet light. If the filter is perfect, you will not be able to see the light, because ultra-violet rays, when unadulterated by other rays, cannot be seen by the human eye. There. The light is on.

"I have offered evidence to Sergeant McGinty in which I intended to prove that Biggert, William Weedham's secretary, was killed because he was about to show to William Weedham a check to which William Weedham's signature had been forged. Not only that, but the forger, in cashing the check, also forged the endorsement of Major Paxton, to whom the check was made out.

"I have further pointed out to McGinty, that this same killer disposed of Jack Carlson, after Carlson had been betrayed by a woman. This woman must have been Carlson's friend. She must have known all his secrets, including the fact that Carlson was the Eye. She gave all this information to another man—the same man who forged the check which I mentioned before. Then she assisted this killer to shoot Carlson. This woman's face powder was treated with naphthionate of sodium. A little of this powder rubbed from her cheek to Carlson's lapel made Carlson a perfect target in pitch darkness, provided that darkness was penetrated by rays of invisible ultra-violet or black light. I have a sample of that woman's face powder here on McGinty's desk."

Black Hood turned the ultra-violet lamp on the desk. The box of powder there became phosphorescent.

"When I was framed for the Tauber jewel robbery tonight, I seized the opportunity to toss some of this face powder onto the jewels in the robbers' bag," Black Hood continued. "The face powder is that of Vida Gervais. Watch, please."

Black Hood turned the ultra-violet lamp out toward his audience. Vida Gervais' frightened face glowed in the black light. Startled gasps could be heard from the others in the room as they stared at that ghostly face.

"Vida Gervais," Black Hood continued, "knew a good thing when she saw it. To eventually better her social and financial position, she was willing to sell out Carlson, alias the Eye, to another man who, if he could accumulate, through fair means or foul, quite a tidy sum of money now would get his hands on a great deal more money in the future.

"So Vida Gervais betrayed Carlson, alias the Eye, into the hands of the man who had killed Biggert. The forty thousand dollars which this man had got from the forged check was a small part of the money he needed. But if he could step into the Eye's shoes for a little while, he could rapidly accumulate the rest.

"I mentioned a moment ago that I had tossed some of Vida Gervais' unusual face powder onto the diamonds stolen from Tauber's shop. The naphthionate in that powder would cling to the diamonds and subsequently cling to the hands of the criminal who eventually got hold of them. Watch now for the glowing hands of the killer—the man who has been impersonating the Eye ever since Carlson was killed. But one funny thing about that impersonation which I did not realize until tonight. The impersonator, this man who killed Biggert and Carlson, was most careful to avoid any word or name beginning with the letter 'D.' He would not, for instance, say the name 'Delancy,' nor would he speak the word 'diamonds.' Why? Because every time he says a word or name beginning with that letter, he stutters. He might disguise his voice by whispering, but he could not control this stutter, which would have been a dead giveaway."

IN THE black light, luminous fingers suddenly showed themselves. There was a piercing scream. Men surged forward to close in and blot out the glow from the killer's fingers.

"Watch out!" Black Hood's warning voice rang out. "He is probably armed!"

Men bumped into each other. There was the repeated thud of blows. There were cries, grunts, stammered oaths. And when finally somebody turned on the lights, Jeff Weedham was on the floor, two cops astride him. He had a gun in his hand, but his hand was pinned to the floor.

Sergeant McGinty looked over his shoulder at the Black Hood—or rather looked where he thought the Black Hood would be. McGinty's jaw sagged. He looked down at his own gun which was poking him in the ribs. His revolver had been wedged into the baby-gate extension arm of his own desk telephone. And Black Hood was gone.

It was an hour later that McGinty and his men, by playing Vida Gervais and Jeff Weedham, one against the other, got a full confession which corresponded very closely to Black Hood's reconstruction of the crimes. Jeff Weedham had been placed in rather a desperate position by his father, Jeff explained. William Weedham had bought Jeff the newspaper, insisting that he make a financial success of it and thus prove his worth. If he failed in this as he had in everything else, William Weedham was determined that none of the Weedham fortune should fall into Jeff's hands.

Jeff had run his newspaper into the red. As the time came closer in which William Weedham was to examine the newspaper's ledger, Jeff Weedham tried desperately to make up the lost money, first by forgery, and then by stepping into Carlson's shoes as the Eye.

Ballistics tests proved that it was Jeff's gun which had killed both Biggert and Carlson.

Just as McGinty was about to leave his office for the night, his phone rang. Almost before he picked the instrument up, he knew who his caller was.

"I say, McGinty," the voice of the Black Hood came from the receiver, "I really intended to apologize for making a fool of you there in your office, sticking you up with a gun attached to that telephone arm. But then, as I thought the matter over, it occurred to me that I really wasn't to blame for making a fool of you. You've really got a bone to pick with dear old Mother Nature on that score!"

"Say, will you kindly go to Hell!" McGinty exploded. And as he hung up, a chuckle broke from his thick lips. "What that guy don't know is that I'm beginning to get a kick out of tangling with him!"

CANDIDATE FOR A COFFIN
By T. W. FORD

Wilson Lamb cuddled his automatic to play "Mr. Death" and fingered little Louis Engel for coffin cargo. But when he pulled the trigger, Whisper, the gun-cobra from Chi, spilled out of Doom's deck. . . . .

DEATH STOOD on the Times Square subway platform, uptown side, waiting for a subject. Death looked at himself in the gum machine mirror, then down at his watch. It was exactly 4:12 P. M., Wednesday, December 10th. When the second hand hit the "30" mark, he would turn around and the person nearest would be It. Death wore a blue pin-stripe suit, well fitting but slightly unpressed. Death's name was Wilson Lamb.

The second hand wiped over the "20" of the smaller dial, jittered on toward the half-minute spot. Inexorable and meaningless. Just as what Wilson Lamb planned. He said "Now" with a little sucking in of breath and a thin anticipant smile and spun on his heel. He was a slim saturnine-faced man with cigaret-ash stain on a coat lapel.

Undistinguished from any typical strap-hanger except perhaps by the light-hued eyes. His shoes needed a shine. He lifted the pale eyes from them and looked for the corpse to be. To the left. To the right. Then he came as near recoiling from the thing as he ever would.

It looked as if it might be a woman. Somehow he had always thought of killing a man. Something that could strike back. Not that he would get the chance. It was just the idea of the thing. But she, the woman, was descending the stairs that led up to the shuttle, bearing down toward him, less than twenty feet away. Big and billowy and red-faced, waddling along like a sow. To face a jury, charged with doing away with a hunk of human beef like that and—

He flashed a glance to the left again. Nobody near. It was a fluke of circumstance a score of people weren't buzzing all about him. He whipped his eyes back toward the woman as a local thundered in. And Luck took a hand. A stocky man dodged around from behind the woman and came rapidly down the platform, neat, crisp, briefcase under his arm.

Wilson Lamb's pale eyes flickered with amusement. He said softly, "Tag, you're it, John W. Goon." This was his corpse to be. Mr. Death had made his pick-up.

"*Ex*-cuse me." An express rolled in and cutting over for it, the stocky man brushed Lamb. His voice was mild, colorless. He wore a gray snap-brim hat; it was set squarely on his head, precisely level. Lamb had seen hats worn like that by show-window clothing dummies. The man entered the third car, middle door. Wilson Lamb boarded it on his heels.

His victim almost got a seat. A pimply-faced office boy elbowed him out of it and the man turned away meekly. He hooked himself onto a strap, hitched the briefcase up under his free arm, and concentrated on a segment of his folded-open newspaper. It was one of the conservative sheets, comic-less, reactionary Republican to the core. Wilson eased down the aisle, casually pushing a woman out of his way, and glanced over his victim's shoulder. The goon was studying an advertisement for a nine-piece living room suite, overstuffed, at "special reduction this week only." It was at one of the better department stores.

Amusement flickered in Wilson Lamb's

pale eyes. He got the picture. A typical George Babbitt in the flesh. To the core.

At Seventy-second Street, the stocky man got a seat. When he faced the light, Lamb saw that he was turning slightly gray over the ears. He had a roundish face, a little fleshy under the chin, a soft-lipped mouth that from habit he held slightly pursed, muddy eyes. He was inclined to plumpness. Somebody had scuffed his right shoe in getting out and now he pulled up the pant leg of his dark grey suit to study it ruefully.

"Typical taxpayer," Lamb said to himself, savoring it. "Always makes his insurance payments on time. . . . Probably has weak arches. . . . Is going to buy the Five Foot book-shelf, always next week, and read it. . . . Would like to get up nerve enough to take that blonde steno at the office out to luncheon. . . ." Wilson Lamb wanted to laugh out loud; it was as good as having a duck flutter down smack in front of your blind.

Past 86th, the Express roared. Lamb's victim had turned his paper, halved back the last page. Automatic pencil poised, he was scanning the crossword puzzle intently. As they lolled through 91st, he bared his teeth in a satisfied smile and rapidly filled in four vertical blanks, then filled out the lower right-hand corner. Lamb saw that his four upper front teeth were a neatly fitted denture. He wondered how they'd look after a bullet had gone through them.

The victim got off at 96th, carefully straightening his muffler inside his black overcoat. He went downstairs, crossed beneath the local platform to the west side, mounted to street level. He had a cigaret in his mouth but waited until he was outside the subway entrance before he put a match to it. Lamb lit one too. He picked up an evening paper from the newsstand —it might come in handy if he got to close quarters with the dope and wanted to mask his face. The newsdealer was looking the other way as he made change so Lamb plucked back his nickel.

THE victim started to cross 96th Street, heading north. A traffic officer's whistle shrilled. Broadway was spattered with the ruby red of traffic lights. Vehicles moved crosstown. Dutifully Lamb's goon turned and retraced his steps to the curb, holding his four-square hat carefully. A little trick with skimpy skirts whipped about plump calves crossed on over. Watching her, Lamb's victim shook his head.

Lamb could hear him saying: "Tsk! Tsk! Foolish to take chances like that." Imagine him saying it, anyway.

Lamb kept at a cautious distance as they moved several blocks up Broadway. Walking briskly, the victim turned into a side street. There was something smug about the way he picked up his heels, swung his briefcase.

"Little man who has had a busy day with a job well done," Lamb paraphrased it sarcastically. He pushed his battered felt hat further back on his head in a gesture of disgust. His cheap unbuttoned raglan-style coat fluttered in the wind off the Hudson. Abruptly, the man ahead halted, wheeled.

Lamb calmly turned and opened the rear door of a parked sedan whose driver was at the wheel. Put a foot in. Down the block, his victim headed into a distinctly second-rate apartment hotel. Lamb said to the sedan driver, "I thought this was a hearse" and went down the block.

His victim was getting his mail at the desk when Lamb entered the shabby lobby. Lamb got on the elevator after him. The victim said "nine," immersed in his paper again, studying that living room suite. He had his key ready in his hand, terra cotta-hued tab swinging loose. "914" was lettered on it in black.

"Ten, Bud," Lamb told the operator.

On the tenth floor, he moved quickly down the frayed carpet of a corridor and found the service stairs. Back on the ninth, even when he was yards from the door of 914, he caught the odor of cooking. Rich and greasy. He got his ear against the door.

"Spare-ribs and sauerkraut, huh, Ede?" the victim was calling out inside. Lamb could visualize him putting his coat on a hanger, carefully folding a scarf over it.

From the rear of the apartment came Ede's voice, reedy and with a bit of a whine. Lamb could visualize her too, a dyed blonde who devoured film fan magazines and thought the girdle was the world's greatest invention. "Uh-huh. How'd things go downtown today, Lou?"

Through the thin door, Lamb heard him clear his throat, mutter, "Oh, so-so."

But Ede wasn't to be put off. "Lou, did you tell the boss you had to have a raise, that the job is worth more?"

Lou started to mumble something. Ede's voice, penetrating the door easily, rose to a querulous pitch. "Lou, you're too easy-going! You ain't got the sense to stand up for your rights. You're an expert in your line and you know it. There's never any kick-back or complaint on a job you do."

"I know, I know, Ede but—" Wilson Lamb's victim got in.

"You're entitled to more money, Lou! You've never bungled a job yet. I need a new coat. And you said you wanted to put the kid in a private school after the first of the year. How're we gonna do it if you don't—"

Lou said, "Look, Ede! Something came up today and the boss had to leave in a hurry—right in the middle of a conference. I just had time to grab my briefcase myself. Let's get to work on those spare-ribs."

They moved toward the rear of the apartment and Lamb out in the hall could hear no more. He was chuckling as he walked away, loose mouth curled in a sneer. Back on the tenth floor, he boarded the elevator again. Again it was empty except for the operator, a tow-headed kid with a Racing Form tucked in a side pocket.

"Funny thing," Lamb mentioned casually, "I could've sworn I knew that man who rode up with me. Stocky chap. Got off at the ninth. But I can't seem to recall his name."

"Mr. Engel, yuh mean?"

"Engel . . . Engel . . . Lou Engel? Is he an accountant?"

"Yeah, Louis Engel's the name. But he ain't no accountant. Comes from Chicago. I heard him tell the manager he was an efficiency expert."

Lamb stopped rattling the coins in his pocket suggestively, kept them there, and strolled toward the main entrance. Behind him, a lobby lounger moved over to the elevator boy, jerking his chin in Wilson Lamb's direction as he asked a question.

At the corner, Lamb stopped in and bought a drink. Thin face creased in a smile of self-satisfaction, he glanced at the paper he had bought. Below the latest war communiques was a small column-head about a threatened gang war in the numbers racket. "Police Raid Joe 'The Flasher'

Abadirro's Headquarters," it said. Lamb's eyes picked up flashes of it. ". . . when plainclothes squad walked into luxurious apartment . . . midtown West Side hotel . . . several henchmen taken into custody on technical charges . . . Abadirro reported out of town . . . police acting on tip killers imported from Chicago . . . showdown anticipated on who will boss numbers racket in metropolitan area. . . ."

LAMB turned the paper over and winked at himself in the concave mirror of the semi-circle of bar. That was unimportant claptrap to somebody like him. That kind of tripe was for the little Joe Dopes who got their thrills vicariously. There was going to be nothing vicarious about what he was going to do. He was going to rub out Louis Engel. Blast him. Louis the Goon, as he had already christened him in his mind. He had put the finger on him.

"Louis the Goon is going to die," Wilson Lamb said softly. He liked the sound of it.

He wasn't crazy. Long ago he had assured himself of that. It was just that his mind operated on a different, a higher, plane than the norm. He was not one of the little pieces of protoplasm running along with the herd. He was above them. Looking down on them. Studying them. His perspective ranged somewhat further than the end of his nose, the latest double-feature at the neighborhood movie house, and spare-ribs.

That last made him laugh out loud. He picked up his change and headed back for the subway and his two-room apartment in the Village. His gun, a .45 automatic, was there. He would be needing it soon. Louis the Goon practically demanded, invited, the use of a .45 automatic on him.

"Efficiency engineer," Lamb said to himself once.

The guy was the perfect subject. Ripe for murder. The more Lamb thought of it, the more he was convinced he couldn't have dreamed up a better stooge. Engel was a model—for homicide. He himself might die for it.

But that was unimportant. The killing of Louis the Goon was the only thing that counted. The results, materially speaking, meant nothing. This slaying was to be an exposition of the ego. Without other cause. Emotionless. With no hope of gain, financial or otherwise. No female involved. Nothing. Just a killing, a plain open and shut case of homicide for no earthly reason imaginable to the police. It would be amusing to watch those flatfoots sitting around trying to sift a motive out of the thing. Baby, they'd sweat their so-and-so's off trying to cook up a reason for this one.

It was so simple to Lamb himself. Inevitable. A logical step in a sequence. The final step, perhaps. Louis the Goon Engel was a mere walk-on in the piece, a spear-carrier doomed to death. Little better than a papier mache dummy set up to be a target for the custard pie. Only, in this case, the custard pie was to be a cupro steel-nosed bullet.

To Lamb, it boiled down to an ultimate expression of the psyche. The final test of one's ability to project the personal ego over all else in the material world. Because the ego was the alpha and omega of all living the moment one got above the level of animal existence, the mere feeding of the face and satisfaction of the other instinctive physical hungers. As Braunitsch had put it so succinctly, "Even the lowest worm can procreate itself—unfortunately."

Then, of course, there was Neitsche and his superman. And some of Freud. And that treatise of Van de Water, the Belgian, on the sublimation of the sub-conscious by the negation of the self-censor. And the papers of Braulinski of the old University of Warsaw on the fear trauma which he termed a birthmark of civilization. Lamb had gone into them all, deeply. All of them dealing with the ego. The ego and its development and complete consummation. And the killing of Louis the Goon Engel was going to be the consummation of Wilson Lamb's experiments in the total exemplification of that ego.

It was no brash idea, no hare-brained impulse concocted in one's cups, perhaps. Analytically, objectively, he had thought out the whole thing. The axis of life was the psyche. Its two poles were birth and death. And, as Braunitsch had stated, the former was a function, often accidental, of which the lowest animal order was capable. A mono-cell, the amoeba, was able to reproduce itself by the simple stratagem of subdivision. But death—when it became a deliberate action, administered without emotion or hope of material gain—was one step removed from the godhead. Perhaps less than one step. But the step that would raise one above all the little fumbling, blind-spawning, life hugging bipeds who infested the scene.

In short, birth was fortuitous, a product of circumstance plus proximity, its get a biological accident. But death—the taking of life— was a selective process, intentionally executed, the result a foreseen conclusion. In so doing, the taking of life, you broke the greatest law of humanity and so became above it. You unfettered the ego with a single ineradicable stroke. In taking a life, one tasted the essence of living. He tried to remember who had said that. De Maupassant had put it better but Lamb could not quite recall the quotation. . . .

He was still trying to remember it as he lounged down the block from Engel's apartment hotel at 8:10 the next morning. There was a bone-chilling breeze off the Drive that made Lamb belt his coat tighter about him. When, at 9:35, Louis the Goon Engel had not made an appearance, Lamb went down to the corner drugstore and had a cup of coffee. He could not see the entrance of the hotel through the window. But he commanded a clear view of the street and anybody coming up it toward the subway. And if he ever saw one, his corpse-to-be was a methodical little piece of humanity. He would come and go to the subway by the same route.

WILSON LAMB was correct as he had never doubted. But it was 11:07 by his wrist watch before Engel emerged. The gray hat just as squarely set on his head as before, without a glance around, Engel came out of the hotel and turned his steps dutifully in the direction of the subway. Lamb was strolling on the other side of the street at the moment. On sight of him, he turned up the front stairs of a brownstone. But a few seconds later, his long legs were carrying him rapidly toward Broadway. By hustling, he got to the other side of it, entered the subway on the uptown side, crossed underneath and was waiting in the by-pass when Engel came along. Engel trotted up to the downtown express platform. When the next train pulled out, Lamb was in the vestibule, half a car-length away from him.

Taking the trouble to keep at a distance, to make himself inconspicuous, seemed almost wasted effort. Louis the Goon went along, looking neither to right nor left,

docilely intent on minding his own business.

"Efficiency expert," Lamb said to himself. "Bet he's a cracker-jack at cutting down on the overhead."

It was like playing a game of cat-and-mouse with him, Wilson Lamb, the cat. Only in this instance, the mouse seemed as good as blind.

Lamb could have given it to him any time, a slug in the back that would terminate his little life the way you would step on a cockroach. On second thought, he would not give it to him in the back. It would be the front so he could see the stricken stupid look of surprise. He'd probably try to get his foolish little briefcase in front of him like a shield. Lamb could just see it. Hear his squeal of futile protest, too.

Yes, he could give it to him whenever he chose. Just walk up to him and squeeze the trigger and savor omnipotence for a moment. Very simple. At his leisure. But Wilson Lamb wasn't going to do it that way. That would have been like a blind stab in the dark, meaningless, impersonal. Like taking a hack at a piece of meat. Or tossing a bomb into a crowd. Instead, he wanted to know something about his specimen before he exterminated him. Understand his background. Get a fair picture of the little sphere of the life from which he was all unknowingly about to depart.

Lamb didn't figure it to take long in the case of Louis the Goon. What Engel was was pretty patent. A typical little tax-payer, careful to keep his nose clean, asking only to be permitted to tread his narrow path unmolested. Undoubtedly the type who got sick to his stomach at the sight of blood even though it might be no more than a nose-bleed.

At 42nd Street, Louis the Goon got off and trundled over to the shuttle. He passed through the Grand Central Station, stopping off to buy a package of Camels en route. The cigar store had a counter display of a bargain buy of razor blades combined with some unknown brand of shaving cream. Engel hovered over it like a bargain-hunting housewife. The clerk put on his spiel. Engel bought, got stuck for a bottle of after-shave lotion too.

Lamb saw it all from over by the counter of the baggage-checking room. " 'A penny saved is a penny earned,' " he paraphrased for him.

They cut through the Graybar Building

to come out on Lexington. Engel pro-
ceeded north a few blocks, turned into one
of the commercial hotels noted for its name
band. Halfway across the lobby, a tall
swarthy man with one of those deadpan
faces rose to greet him. They shook hands.

"You're right on the dot," the tall man
said.

Engel's pursed mouth lengthened in a
flattered smile. "I always make it a point
to be punctual," Lamb dawdling in the
background, overheard him say.

Then they headed for the elevator bank.
The tall one shot two glances backward
as they did so Lamb couldn't make it too
obvious. When he rounded the corner of
the ell where the elevators were, they were
gone. Lamb went back into the main lobby
and ensconced himself behind a morning
paper. Midway down the page was more
about the threatened strife in the numbers
racket. It didn't interest Lamb in the
slightest.

Engel probably had gone upstairs to try
and peddle one of his efficiency schemes to
some big shot. The guy he'd met in the
lobby was a go-between, doubtlessly. Lamb
wondered whether Louis the Goon would
get up the nerve to hit his boss for that
raise today, as Ede had demanded.

Lamb almost lost him. Half an hour
later. Louis the Goon came down and
scooted out the side entrance in a hurry.
When Lamb got out there, his man was
already in a cab, shooting away. There
was something wrong about the conservative, penny-saving Engel taking a taxi.
Wilson Lamb did not realize it at the time.

They went westward across town. Over
near Sixth, Lamb's driver lost the other
cab. Lamb was cursing when he spotted
Engel on the sidewalk, coming back across
town. That was strange because he could
have sworn Engel's cab had not stopped.
Must have gotten it mixed up with another. Out, he threaded his way recklessly
through a welter of vehicles and picked up
the tail as his man entered an office building.

It was fairly crowded in that foyer and
it was simple to step onto the elevator right
at Louis the Goon Engel's back, then wheel
behind him out of sight as he turned. Engel
called "Fourteen" and got out there, briefcase tightly clutched up under his arm, its
flap unbuckled.

"GOING in to high-pressure somebody on a sale," Lamb figured.

Another passenger had called fifteenth,
the next floor. Lamb got out there, found
the built-in fire escape, and got down to
fourteen. This was a little foolish, he
realized. There was no way of finding
what office Louis the Goon had visited.
Still, he might see him when he came out.
Maybe he had gone to see the boss about
that raise Ede was demanding. Maybe he'd
come out bouncing on his tail-feathers. It
was fun following and watching Louis the
Goon. Like watching an ant on a sidewalk flagstone puttering about its puny
business, knowing you were going to stamp
out its life when it so pleased you.

Lamb was just lighting a cigaret, gazing
down the hallway of the fourteenth floor,
when the muffled report came up the stair-
case. It didn't seem possible, a gun seemed
so out of place in such surroundings. . . .
Then there were two more shots, a scream
intermixed. The shattering of plate glass.
Lamb was down the stairs and pulling open
the fire-door onto the floor below. Immediately he sniffed the acrid fumes of gun-
powder.

He was looking out onto an ell of that
floor. Onto a tableau of violence. There
was just a single office suite on that ell,
directly opposite him. On one of its
double doors was lettered "Continental Exhibition Corp." The frosted glass of the
other door was almost completely broken
out, leaving a jagged-fringed aperture
through which to view the scene within.

Wilson Lamb flattered himself on being
pretty cool headed under all circumstances.
But he blinked three times rapidly now.
Inside the Continental Exhibition Corporation one man was slumped over a desk, an
automatic half-gripped in his inert hand.
He was very dead. Half his head was shot
off. Another man was sprawled on the
gray broadloom of the reception room, a
brownish puddle beneath his side. He
wasn't going to be going any place in a
hurry, either.

Even as Lamb stared at the carnage, a
third figure appeared, wobbling drunkenly
from an inner office. He came stooped
over, holding his side. Crimson-speckled
froth at his lips. He got to the shattered
glass panel and moved the lips at Wilson
Lamb.

"Tell 'em—the police—it was—was
Whisper Ross from—from Chi—" He
coughed twice on the "Chicago," then

caved in on himself and went flat in the hallway.

Lamb saw an ashen-face bespectacled man peering around the corner of an ell. From further back, through an open doorway, a girl's voice was shrieking for the police over the phone. Lamb remembered the fact that he had a gun on his person. It might be extremely embarrassing if the police picked him up for questioning. Ducking back through the firedoor, he ran quickly up to the sixteenth floor, up past the fifteenth. Nothing had been heard up there yet. He caught a down car and got out just as the first prowl car came sirening its way into the side street curb.

Afterward, outside the police cordon thrown around the building, somebody jostled against him, peered under his hat brim. Later, Lamb recalled the bluish scar crescent on his left cheek.

"Hey, aren't you Reynolds of the Dispatch, pal?"

"Nope," Lamb said.

"You're a reporter with one of the local sheets, aren't you?" the other persisted. "I know I've seen you around before."

"You must have been wearing your other glasses, Bud," Lamb said and turned away.

Maybe it was the effect of seeing the handiwork of that other unknown killer. For the police had nabbed nobody yet in that mid-town mid-day shooting. Anyway, Lamb had the itch to strike. It was like a thirst building in a guy. You've seen somebody else dip into a tall cool one and after a while you feel like you got to have one yourself. Those three dead men on the thirteenth floor of that office building had acted like an aphrodisiac on Wilson Lamb. He wanted to get him his corpse. But soon.

He knew it when he picked up his victim again. It was almost 4 P.M., shreds of snow drifting down through New York's early darkness. He was hanging around by the cab stand above 96th on the west side of Broadway, waiting hopefully. He had got so that he felt a little lonely when he didn't have Louis the Goon right handy. He felt on familiar terms with the guy. Of course, Louis the Goon didn't know him. And when he introduced himself, Louis was going to get one hell of a big surprise. Like a kick in the teeth only a lot more permanent.

One of the hackies turned up his radio.

A news commentator was on. He came to the topic of the mid-town shooting. Three dead, gunned in the office of the Continental Exhibition Corporation. Lamb edged over nearer. The Continental outfit, the announcer said, was the business front of one Big John Girra, well known local racketeer. Girra was a powerful figure in the metropolitan pin-ball game syndicate and had a piece of the number policy racket too.

"Police, promising an arrest within twenty-four hours, claim the triple killing a step in the fight for control of the numbers game business in this city. They are still seeking the missing Joe The Flasher Abadirro, also reputed to have boasted he would take over the numbers game. Two of the slain men have been identified as close associates of Big John Girra. A building employee stated earlier today that Girra left the premises less than five minutes before the killing. A prominent police official who refused to be quoted asserted the killer was a Chicago torpedo imported for the job, a killer who would not be recognized by members of the New York mobs. 'We are closing in on him at this very instant,' the official concluded."

THE news broadcaster went on to another item of the day's reports. Lamb turned around. And there was Louis the Goon Engel, not four feet away. En route home from the subway, he had paused to listen to the report too. He stood now with a calculating look, almost as if he were checking the verity of the report. Lamb wanted to laugh in his face.

"If you'd seen those three carcasses leaking blood all over the place, you'd probably have swooned in your britches, my little dope," Lamb addressed him mentally. And the funny part was that the little dope had been so close to it. Just a floor away, in fact.

As he followed him on uptown, down his side-street, Lamb had a curious sense of elation. He was in on the ground-floor of Death, Inc. Even before voting at a stock-holders' meeting himself. For he knew who had triggered those three today, who the Chi torpedo the cops wanted was. One Whisper Ross. Of course, he might have tipped off the police say, by a phone call. But he wasn't going to.

"We killers must stick together." The thought tickled his sense of humor.

They were almost at Louis the Goon's roost when Lamb saw how he was going to do it. A boy with a carton of groceries almost ran down Louis, then ducked down into the delivery entrance of the apartment-hotel. And Wilson Lamb had his cue.

Some ten minutes later, after due investigation, he knew how he was going to put Louis the Goon on the spot. And how he was going to get away with it, get clear afterward. The taking of life was the important thing, the major premise. Whether he was caught or not had never seemed important before. But after reviewing the handiwork of Whisper Ross—who had ambled off unimpeded — Lamb saw no reason why he should not do the same. It would be the nth degree in the epitomization of the ego to kill and get away with it.

The building's delivery entrance was a perfect avenue of escape. Actually it did not enter the hotel at first. Down a few steps and then it ran rearward between the side of the building and the retaining wall next door, an open-topped alleyway. The delivery doorway was in the rear. A few feet further on was the backyard laid out in a garden with a waterless age-browned concrete fountain in the center. A low concrete wall separated it from the property that backed onto it. And there was the payoff.

Ambling casually through in the darkness, Lamb had discovered that the property in the rear, facing on the next street downtown, was several feet lower. It would be simple to drop over the wall to its paved courtyard. And from that ran a concrete passage beside the apartment house out to the street one block below.

Emerging on it, Lamb lit a cigaret and went back around the block to Engel's place. He appraised it like a surveyor. First off, it was one of those second-rate places that boasted no doorman. Across the street were those brownstones for a nice dim background. The nearest street lamp was down about ten feet from the entrance of Engel's place. Engel would come walking along primly, right into its light. A man crossing the street from the brownstones, a little behind Engel, calling out, "Hey, Mr. Engel," and—

It was a very nice setup. The property line of the building where Engel lived was set back several feet further than that of the old-fashioned private homes between it and Broadway. They would serve as a

screen for his movements from one direction when he hit into that delivery alleyway after fixing Louis the Goon's wagon once and for all, Lamb realized. It was almost ridiculously simple.

Why he could almost have chalked an "X" right there and then on the sidewalk where little Louis would lie down and forget it all. Wilson Lamb hummed as he headed up toward Broadway and decided to have dinner. He had a swell appetite. He was humming snatches from something. Minor key, descending scale. It went "Come to Papa, come to Papa, come to Papa." He didn't know whether it was from a song or a crap game. Anyway, the dice were sure loaded against a certain party he knew.

Down the block, a taxi that had been parked with meter ticking across from Engel's apartment-hotel drew away slowly.

He went to the movies with Louis the Goon that evening. Louis didn't know anything about it and Lamb bought his own ticket. That too had been extremely simple. After dinner, he had phoned Engel. When Louis himself answered, Lamb had asked for Toots. Louis said they had no Toots there and Lamb said he was very sorry, that he must have got the wrong number. And Louis said that was all right, no harm done. And Lamb said he was sorry he had disturbed him and Louis said to think nothing of it, no trouble at all. And Lamb said a four-letter word after he had hung up and laughed out loud in the phone booth.

Then he hung around and saw Louis come out after dinner. Ede was with him this time. Ede was the type after which some department store advertising-department diplomat had coined the term "stylish stout." Ede toddled and she was pretty hefty. If there was a family argument, Lamb would have laid two to one she would have come home in front by a t.k.o. before the fifth round.

THEY went into the movies on the northwest corner of 96th. The closest Lamb could get was some three rows back. He was disappointed because he could not watch Engel's face. It was a double feature. *Pampas Nights* was one of those alleged South American musicals whipped up by a couple of submorons with the intent purpose of sabotaging the Good Neighbor policy. The other picture was some ghoulish thing about a mad surgeon, described in the script as an "ego-maniac," who had a pleasant pastime of revivifying electrocuted felons. That one gave Lamb a pain in the pants too. He had really made a study of ego-maniacs.

He got out in the foyer right behind the Engels. He heard Ede say she thought the one about that "nutty doc" was so thrilling. Louis the Goon did not agree. He liked those musicals.

"They take my mind off business," he said.

Lamb left them and went in and had a drink. He had two drinks. Now that everything was settled, he felt no impatience. It was all lined up right down to the final curtain. Louis' final curtain. Lamb had already decided he would give it to him as he came plodding his smug little way home some evening. Any evening. Maybe tomorrow evening. Now that the details were ironed out, it was fun to leave the closing date open. He could pay the fly-on-the-wall in Louis the Goon's life as long as he wanted. And when he got bored with Louis's act—bop! he would deliver his compact little package to Louis. . . .

He started to get bored fast the next day. He rode downtown with Louis and they went over to that same East side hotel and Louis went upstairs. He was gone a long time. Lamb said to himself, "That dope goes around in a rut and I'll get in one too just following him and then I will get sore." Eventually Louis the Goon came back down into the lobby. The tall, swarthy man he had met there the day before was with him.

"Well, I guess there'll be nothing doing today," Louis the Goon said.

"Nope, nothing," the other said.

They parted. Louis went down to the telephones, used one after consulting a little black book. When he came out, he bought a white carnation for his buttonhole in the florist shop, then treated himself to three twenty-five-center Perfectos.

"Something builds," Lamb told himself. Outside, when Louis the Goon got a taxi, there was something positively cocky about him. Lamb was humming his "Come to Papa" again as he took another and trailed him eastward this time. Louis got out at a Third Avenue bar and grill and went in. Lamb gave him five minutes and strayed

in himself. There was no Louis. Not at first, anyway. Lamb could feel his pulse beat faster.

Then he spotted the dim backroom with the booths. And he went through it to the Men's Room. And there was Louis the Goon—his little clay pigeon—in one of the booths with a doll. She was redhaired by courtesy of the local beauty parlor, cuddling up in a flashy little leopard fur number. She looked like a dance-hall hostess from one of those joints where everything goes so long as you keep time to the music.

As Lamb passed, she was saying, "Now, Daddy—" That almost unbuttoned Lamb. Daddy! On his way back, he noticed there were two others in the backroom, a couple of men gnawing on pretzels over beers.

He stepped back into the bar just in time. Three men had entered. They headed straight for the rear. One of them shouldered Wilson Lamb from his path as if he did not see him. The second one pulled out a cannon and poked it at the bartender and told him to keep his britches on. Then the other two were in the rear and letting go with their cannon.

Slammed over against the bar, Lamb had a split-second glimpse of it. For a moment, it almost seemed as if the damn fools were out after Engel. One shot smashed the table lamp in the booth where he sat. Then the two beer drinkers back in there were around and swapping it out with cannon of their own with the newcomers.

Lamb got out of there fast. He got across the street. He saw two men dash out of a side entrance and into a dark sedan that roared away. He did not see Louis the Goon get out. Then the howling prowl cars converged on the scene. And there was an ambulance. It took one guy away. Another guy, it didn't. Lamb worked his way up into the throng and got a glimpse of the other guy getting stiff on the backroom floor. Everybody else was lined up in the bar for questioning. Engel was not among them. So Lamb knew he must have gotten away all right.

"This is some more of that numbers racket war," a gray-haired sergeant said. And then Lamb began to taste something like panic even as the first neon signs began to smear the wintry shadows. He got afraid he might lose his little clay pigeon. Louis the Goon seemed to have a blind genius for getting on the scene when some blood-letting was due. He felt a certain possessiveness toward Louis. Louis belonged to him. And he wasn't going to have him chopped down by any piece of stray lead. Lamb had a bullet ear-marked for Louis.

HE said, "I've been wasting time." He got on the shuttle and over to the West side and up to 96th and across the street from where Louis lived. Well, where Louis used to live, anyway. He was there just twenty minutes—it was 4:43 by his wristwatch—when Louis the Goon came down from the corner. He couldn't make out his face at first but he knew him by that square-set hat. Lamb eased away from the stairs of the brownstone, humming "Come to Papa, come to Papa, come to Papa. . . ." This was it.

The ultimate in the demonstration of the ego. . . . He told himself that as he moved over the scabrous snow of the street. . . . The zenith in the projection of the psyche. . . . Louis the Goon had his briefcase clutched up under one arm instead of swinging. . . . The final triumph over the fear trauma. . . . Louis was abreast of him, then passing by. Wilson Lamb brought the automatic out from under his coat. He called, "Mr. Engel—" And Louis the Goon turned and Lamb held it, wanting him to get a good look at the heater, wanting to get a good look at him as he saw it.

Engel had the briefcase open, unbuckled. He was bringing something out of it swiftly, jerkily. It was a heater too. That wasn't in the script. Louis the Goon was stepping out of role. But Lamb knew he had him anyway and started to squeeze. He would squeeze three times on that trigger and—

Somebody else squeezed first. It was the man running from that parked car down the street. Lamb got it in the side and then a red-hot finger was probing down

into his guts. A man stepped from the vestibule of one of those brownstones and he squeezed and Wilson Lamb couldn't feel the side of his head any more. Knew he would never feel it again. He was down on one hand and one knee and his gun was gone. Some place in the black haze seething around him. Like a hurt animal, half crawling, knowing only the base instinct of self preservation, he tried for that delivery alleyway.

Somebody else had figured that was a good spot too. It was the man with the bluish cheek scar who had accosted him after the triple-killing in that office building. He squeezed. And Lamb took that one square on the chest. In a vague way, as the sidewalk slid up at him, he was aware of that car back-firing away like hell.

The man with the blue scar was standing over him, throwing words to Louis the Goon in a quick, harsh whisper. "This is the one, Whisper. He come in here with you Wednesday. He was on the spot when you give it to them boys in Girra's office, yesterday. Today, he was in that bar when they tried to get you. The Flasher said to stick close to you—an' him."

"Girra's finger man, eh?" called back Engel softly.

"Yeah, Whisper." The blue-scarred man ran. In a moment, a car roared off down the block toward West End Avenue.

Lying there on the sidewalk, blasted for keeps, his wagon fixed, Wilson Lamb tried to put it together. Things moved very slowly for him. Whisper. Whisper Ross, Chi torpedo. Then he had it. Whisper Ross was Louis the Goon Engel. Hired killer of Joe The Flasher Abadirro. The guy he, Wilson Lamb, had fingered for an exposition of his ego.

Down the sidewalk, little Mr. Louis Engel, alias Whisper Ross, stood looking at the body and going "Tsk! Tsk!" through pursed lips. Wilson Lamb's ego died a horrible death seventeen seconds before he did.

ONE HUNDRED BUCKS PER STIFF
by J. LLOYD CONRICH

"THERE'S a guy outside wants to see you, Chief," Charlie Ward's assistant announced through the door.

"What's he want, Joe?"

"I don't know. Says his business is confidential and urgent. Wouldn't say what. Looks harmless though, in spite of he drove up in a Rolls Royce with a chauffeur."

"Well, send him in."

Ward busied himself with a sheaf of morning mail and miscellaneous police circulars. Presently a small, immaculate looking individual with an apologetic, breathless air entered the room and approached the desk timidly. Silently, without even so much as a nod, he laid a newspaper clipping before the Chief of Police. Adjusting his glasses, Ward reached for the item and glanced through it hastily:

MAN KILLED AT EL GATOS
GRADE CROSSING

El Gatos, November 1. The decapitated body of a man tentatively identified as J. Peter Peck, address unknown, was discovered by a company track walker early this morning on the South West Pacific grade crossing half a mile south of the town of El Gatos. Local police believe that the man was killed some time after midnight, possibly by the San Francisco milk train. Identification was established by a wallet containing papers of the deceased.

Ward laid the clipping on his desk, rolled a bulbous wad of chewing tobacco into one cheek and expelled it into a spitoon some ten feet away with a resounding plunk. Wiping his chin inexpertly with the back of a grizzled hand, he looked up and eyed his visitor interrogatively.

"I clipped it from last night's *San Francisco Bulletin*," the latter explained quietly. "I drove practically all night so as to be here this morning."

"You're a relative?"

The stranger smiled weakly and placed a pair of painfully thin hands on the desk as though to steady himself.

"Well, no, not exactly; that is, somewhat," he answered obscurely.

Charlie Ward eyed the little man curiously. "Come again, please?"

"Well, it's this way," slipping nervously to the very edge of a convenient chair. "There appears to have been a slight error made. The clipping is somewhat inaccurate."

"Sure. Half the stuff you see in the papers these days is cockeyed. Them guys never get anything straight. I always tell my wife you gotta believe only ten per cent of what you read and doubt that."

The stranger smiled thinly. "Precisely. Now the real truth of the matter in this particular case is that *I* happen to be J.

Peter Peck and, to the best of my knowledge, I'm not dead. In fact I'd take issue with anyone who questioned the fact. I therefore feel that the report has been exaggerated; just a tiny bit, at least." He paused for breath. "I thought you'd like to know."

Ward arched his brows and smiled calmly. As a veteran police officer, he was used to surprises. "Well, now that's one for the book, ain't it?"

"Rather."

"So, if you're the guy that's supposed to be downstairs on ice," Ward supplemented, fumbling in a drawer of his desk, "how come we find this here wallet with your name all over the papers inside on him?"

Mr. Peck glanced at the wallet.

"Very easily explained," he answered. "I was held up last Monday evening in San Francisco. The wallet and the papers it contains were among the things taken from me. Incidentally, there were several thousands of dollars in the wallet when I last saw it."

Ward whistled softly. "How much?"

"About twenty-four hundred dollars."

"That's a lot of dollars."

"It would keep a man in cigars for a day or two."

"And this guy, after he stuck you up," Ward reasoned, "left Frisco and come North where he had the bad luck to meet with an accident."

"Precisely."

"What'd he look like?"

"There were two of them. One had red hair and his left ear was missing. The other was short; about my size, I would say; rather thin, with a small, black, straggly mustache and swarthy skin. I should judge he were either an Italian or possibly a Spaniard."

"The second one fits the guy on ice. Want to take a squint at him?"

Mr. Peck jumped to his feet.

"I'd be delighted," he said with what sounded to Charlie Ward like unwarranted glee.

Ward picked up a flask of corn whiskey and slipped it into his hip pocket.

"I warn you," he cautioned as he rose, "this guy's pretty much worked over in spots. A train went through him you know. Some people get goose pimples looking at them kind of things."

"I'll risk it."

THE pair left the office and descended a flight of steps. At the end of a dark corridor, Ward led the way into a basement room. Upon one of two marble slabs in the center of the room, lay a sheeted corpse. Ward pulled the shroud back, revealing a horribly mangled body. Mr. Peck leaned over the corpse, revealing none of the repulsion that Ward was sure he would exhibit.

"Yes, that's unquestionably one of the men who held me up," the little man said quietly. "I'd know that face anywhere; what there is left of it. Er—seems to be quite dead, doesn't he?" he added wryly.

"Quite," Ward mimicked, wondering at the same time what strange complex could cause a man of Mr. Pick's evident refinement and good breeding to jest under such circumstances.

The little man leaned over the corpse again.

"Odd marks on his face, aren't they?" he observed.

"Huh?" Ward seemed startled.

"I said those were odd marks on his face," Mr. Peck repeated.

Ward's face clouded and he stepped closer to Mr. Peck.

"It's funny you should notice them red blotches, Mr. Peck," he said. "I been kind of wondering about them myself."

The two men eyed one another for a moment of tense silence, and marked suspicion.

"Why?" Mr. Peck asked abruptly.

Ward scanned the little man's face with an air of uncertainty.

"Er—do them marks mean anything to you?" he finally asked, his voice tinged with caution.

Mr. Peck made no immediate answer, but turned and leaned closer to the corpse, examining the faint red blotches on the cheeks with more care than he had at first taken.

"To the casual observer, that is, to the layman," he said, removing his glasses and facing Ward, "it might appear that the deceased was suffering from a mild case of measles"—he paused, glanced at the corpse again, then turned once more to Ward—"but to the trained eye, I would say that this man has received a shot of xetholine caniopus into his system."

"A shot of what?"

"The name means little. Xetholine caniopus is a drug; not rare, not common, but violently poisonous. Contact, even to the lips or to a flesh abrasion will bring about practically instantaneous paralysis of the cardia." The little man blinked. "Er—the heart, I refer to. Xetholine invariably leaves its mark, as you perceive, in the form of faint red blotches on the cheeks." He thumbed in the direction of the corpse. "Putting the diagnosis into simpler words, this man has been poisoned. He died from the effects of the poison as is indicated by the slight carmine tinge to the blood. The effect of this poison on the blood stream is similar to that caused by asphyxiation by coal gas or a similar substance, only not quite so brilliantly red. If this man had died as a direct result of injuries received by the train passing over his body, the blood would be darker, almost purple. Offhand, I would say that the train passed over his body some several hours after his death. Depending upon the determination as to whether the poison was self administered or otherwise, will settle the question as to whether you have a suicide or a murder case on your hands."

Ward stared into the little man's eyes in astonishment.

"Say," he interrupted, "who are you, anyhow?"

Mr. Peck smiled benevolently.

"My name," he explained, "you already know. I happen to be deeply interested in criminology. It's been an avocation of mine for many years. My specialty is toxicology. I...."

"Tox—tox....?"

"Toxicology; the study of poisons. The circumstances of this particular case are unusually close to home and I feel a personal interest." He paused and peered into Ward's face hesitantly and then added in a voice that half pleaded and half apologized—"I—could I—would you allow me to —er—work with you in this matter, Mr. Ward? I'd expect no pay, of course," he hastened to add, "and I can assure you that my efforts will be sincere and my intentions entirely honorable. My only interest is in clearing up the matter, or at least attempting to do so, for the—well— the fun of doing it."

"Some fun, all right," Ward observed wryly. "But, at that price, the County can't lose much. You're hired."

"That's fine," Mr. Peck enthused, his eyes shining brilliantly. He rubbed his palms together briskly. "I can't tell you how deeply grateful I really am."

"Okay, Mr. Peck," with a shade of doubt. "It's your funeral. The paper says so."

"Now first, I must make a test to satisfy myself that xetholine caniopus was the actual cause of death. There are a few things I'll need; a glass, an ordinary water glass will do, a small quantity of commercial alcohol and a bit of lime water. My chauffeur will get the latter two, if you'll supply the glass. Please notify him."

Ward hesitated, as though doubtful about leaving this unusual person alone in the morgue, but finally assented.

A few minutes later he reappeared with the glass, followed almost directly by the chauffeur with the alcohol and lime water.

"Thank you, Christian," Mr. Peck said in the chauffeur's direction. "You may wait in the car."

WARD'S eyes followed the chauffeur as he left the room.

"He's a big guy all right," he observed, thumbing toward the vanishing driver. "Sure must have et his mush every morning when he was a little boy. Looks like he's about six foot six."

"Six, six and one-eighth in his stocking feet, to be exact," Mr. Peck corrected. "Before meals he weighs two eighty-eight; after meals two ninety-eight."

"Wouldn't want to run into him on a dark night."

"Hardly," Mr. Peck agreed. "When he first came to me, he applied for the position which he now holds under the name of Mike Dennis and explained that he generally answered to the intimate and thoroughly quaint cognomen of 'Butch.' But I changed that to Christian. Of course 'Butch' is more in keeping, but I do believe that Christian adds to his dignity in spite of his ears. Don't you think so?" Ward grunted vaguely. "I have it on good authority that he put Mr. Dempsey to sleep one evening about fifteen years ago in an amateur boxing meet." Mr. Peck's eyes sparkled as he glanced up from his work for a moment. "Unfortunately, I happen to be worth several million dollars. There have been two attempts to abduct me. Christian makes an excellent body guard as well as chauffeur. Not much intellect, but most conscientious and as faithful as an old watch dog. I've had him with me twenty-two months now and to date he's uttered not more than twenty-two words; except, of course, when I speak with him. A handy person to have about; most handy."

By now Mr. Peck had sterilized the glass with the alcohol and was prepared to make his test.

"In the glass," he explained, holding the object toward the light, "I have poured some lime water. By blowing one's breath into the liquid, through a common cigarette holder, the lime water becomes a milky white; thusly," and he suited the action to the word. "The balance of the test is quite simple. Several drops of the deceased's coagulated blood are now added to the water. As you see, there is no change. In a moment, I will add a little alcohol. If the lime water clears and becomes colorless again, and shows indication of a volatile oil on the surface, you may rest assured that xetholine caniopus exists in the blood stream. Although the test is simple, the chemical reaction is rather involved, being a combination and then a dissemination of structural heraetixae and third power phincus. I shall not, therefore, bother you with its details. Suffice to say, the test is infallible and conclusive."

Ward scratched his head in hopeless perplexity and stared in mild anticipation mingled with a great deal of skepticism as Mr. Peck poured a small quantity of alcohol into the glass. Immediately, the liquid became pure and colorless and the surface indicated a distinctly oily film.

"All of which bears me out," Mr. Peck said quietly, placing the glass on the table. "This man has been poisoned. Our next step is to determine whether the poison was self administered or otherwise. We...."

"Just a minute, Mr. Peck," Ward interrupted, raising his hand. "There's a couple of things here I ought to explain." Ward floundered for a moment of hesitancy. "You see, it's this way. For about twenty years, now, about twelve people a year have died in this here town; one a month; that's the average."

"Yes; yes?" Mr. Peck interjected interestedly.

"But in the last month, eleven people have turned in their rain checks. This guy's the twelfth."

"Which more or less upsets the law of averages."

"That's just what I'm getting at. But what's worse, is that ten out of these twelve met with deaths from accidents of one kind or another."

"Just how do you mean?"

"Well, this guy, for instance," motioning toward the slab, "was bumped by a train. The rest met with other accidents ranging all the way from hit and run, down the line to falling off hay lofts and being kicked in the head by a mule. Nobody seen any of the accidents, but the evidence was such that you couldn't help see what happened. For instance, the guy that was kicked by a mule, he had a hoof mark on his head and his mule had a bloody hoof. The hit-run guy, we found in the middle of the highway."

"Coincidence. Accidents almost invariably occur in threes or fours."

"Sure; threes and fours, but not tens and twelves. But there's something else."

" . . . .yes?"

CHARLIE WARD moved a little closer and glanced behind him as he spoke.

"Of the ten who met with accidents," he said, "nine had these red marks on their cheeks."

"Excellent! Gorgeous!" Mr. Peck enthused through grinning lips. "A multiple murder! Nothing could be clearer or more fortunate!"

"Well, you may be tickled, Mr. Peck, but I ain't. Several of the victims were close friends of mine."

Mr. Peck's attitude changed at once.

"I'm deeply sorry, Mr. Ward," he apologized. "My enthusiasm carried me away for the moment. Please proceed."

Ward nodded and went on. "At first I didn't think very much about these blotches, but when this guy was brought in this morning, I began to get kind of nervous. As a matter of fact, I was just going to phone Frisco for help when you come in."

Mr. Peck nodded and smacked his lips thoughtfully. He removed his glasses and wiped them slowly and carefully, polishing each lens with meticulous care.

"You of course have a coroner or medical examiner of some kind," he finally said.

"Oh, sure. Old Doc Kraus handles the cases for the whole county when they come up. There ain't enough to keep him on full time, but we send for him whenever we need him. He makes the examination and runs the inquest."

"What did he think about the red blotches on the faces of the nine corpses?"

"Nothing. To tell you the truth I never thought enough about them to bring it up.

"And he's never mentioned it to you."

"No."

"I can't possibly conceive of anyone missing them."

"The Doc's getting pretty old," Ward explained. "He don't see so good. We been trying to get a younger saw-bones for a long time, but nobody had the guts to tell him he was fired, I guess. He was born here; lived here for seventy-two years. He's a nice enough old guy. Matter of fact, everybody sort of looks up to him as the town granddad. He's a kindly old duffer; always doing things for folks and going out of his way to help a neighbor and things like that. I'll send for him and ask him if he noticed the marks and what he thinks about them."

"No, I'd prefer it if you didn't. For the present, let's work quietly. As far as I'm concerned, everybody's under suspicion and any word getting out that we're working on the case might spoil things."

"Old Doc Kraus under suspicion!" Ward scoffed with a loud guffaw. "Say, that's rich. Why, I'd trust him ahead of my own Dad and that's saying a lot. Why he brought me into this world forty-two years ago. Used to spank me when I was a kid and needed one. Why. . . ."

"I did not say I suspected Doctor Kraus," Mr. Peck interrupted. "I merely inferred that everybody was under suspicion until we begin to find something definite to go on. The reasons, I believe, are obvious."

"I get you Mr. Peck."

"Now then, the inquest has been performed in this last case?"

"Yes; early this morning; just before you got here. They handed down a verdict of accidental death."

"Have you made any attempts to identify the corpse?"

"Certainly. We figured it was you on account of the papers. We been trying to trace you through the Frisco police. So far no information has come in."

"That's quite possible. I lead a very quiet life; live at a bachelor club and am not listed either in the phone book or the City Directory."

"I sent finger prints to the Frisco Police. If this guy's got a record, we'll know who he is pretty quick."

"That's fine."

Mr. Peck stood for a moment with a thoughtful finger to his lips.

"I think we'll visit the spot where the body was discovered," he decided abruptly. "We can go in my car."

TEN minutes later, J. Peter Peck, accompanied by Charlie Ward and followed by Christian, stepped from the machine at a point opposite the spot where the body had been found.

"A machine has stopped here at the side of the road quite recently," Mr. Peck offered, pointing to the tire marks in the dust. "The occupant, as is indicated by those very clear foot prints, stepped from the car, crossed the ditch and walked to the railroad tracks. He was a heavy man, at that, or at least he has big feet. And they turn out more than the feet of the average person."

Charlie Ward nodded agreement.

"Now if you'll look closely," Mr. Peck went on, "you will observe that there are two sets of foot prints; one coming and one going. The return prints, significantly, are not as clear as those that go to the tracks, indicating that he was carrying a load to the tracks, but did not return with it." He glanced at Ward for a moment, then added, "It is pretty obvious what that load was. All of which gives us practically undeniable proof that a murder was committed. The deceased died of poison. We have definitely established that point. And his body was placed upon the tracks to conceal the fact; or to attempt to do so. If the deceased had walked to the tracks himself, which of course he didn't because these are not his foot prints, there obviously would be no return prints. Dead men, especially decapitated dead men, seldom, if ever, retrace their steps." He paused for a moment of conjecture. "We'll take plaster casts of the foot prints as well as the tire marks. Will you attend to that Christian? I believe you'll find sufficient plaster of Paris in the tool compartment."

Christian set to work and Mr. Peck and Ward retreated to the machine. When Christian had completed his work, the trio returned to headquarters, Mr. Peck leaving again to "do a little thinking."

Two hours later, Mr. Peck entered Charlie Ward's office again and eased himself into a chair.

"I have an idea," he informed Ward, "that the apprehension of the murderer is but a matter of moments. As a matter of fact, I can put my finger on him in ten minutes should I care to."

"You can put your finger on him right this minute if you want to," Ward supplemented, taking his feet off the desk and flipping a cigarette butt through the window.

"How so?"

Ward unlocked a drawer in his desk and drew out a tin box from which he produced a thickly padded envelope.

"I been doing a little scientific snooping myself," he announced with a proud ear to ear grin.

"That's extremely gratifying."

Ward thumbed toward a cigar butt in an ash tray.

"That," he said, "is what's left of a cigar you give me this morning. It gives off a pretty thick aroma."

"It ought to. They cost me a dollar each."

"Just take a whiff of this," Ward said, handing the envelope to Mr. Peck.

The latter smelled cautiously. "Why, it smells like my cigars."

"Exactly. Now take a squint in the envelope."

Mr. Peck opened the envelope and extracted a sheaf of currency.

"There's about twenty-four grand there," Ward offered.

"All of which is mine. It's the money that was taken from me when I was held up. I had the wallet and several of the cigars in the same pocket. The currency evidently became impregnated with the odor of the cigars. Where did you get it?"

Ward shuffled leisurely through some papers, finally producing a telegram.

"This wire," he said, flourishing the message with an extravagant gesture, "come in from the Frisco police while you were out. It says the guy downstairs on ice is Dominic Diaz. He was a guest at San Quentin up to four days ago where he was serving ten to fifty years for some mistakes he made when he was younger." Mr. Peck nodded interestedly. "It also says that when he so rudely walked off the premises without stopping to say goodbye, he was with a red headed monkey, minus one ear, that answers to the name of Mike McSweeney."

"I see."

"Mr. McSweeney had the bad taste to try to stick up our local drug emporium about half an hour ago."

"And he is now incarcerated in your bastille."

"Right. And he had your dough on him."

WARD sat back in his swivel chair, hooked his thumbs into the arm holes of his vest and beamed. "Well, I guess that makes it pretty clear. Eh, Mr. Peck? Diaz, the dead pigeon, and this guy McSweeney take it on the lam from the big house. They sticks you up, then blow North and land here. They're going to split, but McSweeney's a pig. He wants the works. So what does he do? He croaks his pal." Ward cocked his head and extended his hands, palms outward. "Okay?"

Mr. Peck scratched his chin thoughtfully.

"Well, fairly so," he answered without enthusiasm. "But before I say *how* clear, I'd like to see this McSweeney person."

A moment later a very sullen and defiant Mike McSweeney was ushered into the room.

"Turn around slowly," Mr. Peck ordered. The man sulked, but with a little persuasion, he finally did as he was told.

"Now take your shoes off."

"Say, what is this, a racket?" the prisoner snarled.

"That will be all," Mr. Peck murmured after a hasty inspection of McSweeney's feet. "You may return him to his cell. And unless you care to have him prosecuted for his attempted robbery of the drug store, you may just as well notify the Warden at San Quentin to come up and get him. His list of crimes, I am sorry to say, Ward, does not include the murder of Dominic Diaz."

"Why—why it's as plain as the nose on your face," Ward spluttered as McSweeney was led from the room. "The cigar smelling currency...."

"You've tried hard," Mr. Peck interrupted, "very hard, in fact. Your efforts are indeed commendable and I do say that your deductions are plausible, but the fact remains that McSweeney is not the man we are looking for."

"Well, couldn't have McSweeney poisoned him and then thrown his body on the tracks?"

"He could have," Mr. Peck conceded, "but there would be no object in attempting to conceal his method of killing his confederate. Besides he is not mentally equipped to think of such things. Offhand, I'd say that his I. Q. is that of an eight year old boy. Remember also, that we are looking for a man—or possibly a woman—who has killed *several* persons within the past thirty days, using the same method; that of the injection of xetholine caniopus. McSweeney couldn't have killed any of the others, for the very simple reason that he has been behind bars up to four days ago."

Mr. Peck raised his hand to silence Ward. "In addition, Mr. Ward, please remember that I have a motor car full of foot print casts. Even in his bare feet, which you saw with your own eyes, he'd overlap those prints a half inch all around. That's why I had his shoes removed. Also, you recall that the man who carried Diaz's body to the railroad tracks possessed feet that pointed outward. McSweeney is decidedly pigeon toed." Mr. Peck raised *his* hands, palms upward, and then dropped them to his chubby knees with a sharp slap. "Now how clear does your case appear?"

Ward grunted and stared out of the window.

"On the other hand, Mr. Ward, as I before stated and now repeat, I can put my finger on the murderer within ten minutes, should I care to."

"Who is it?"

"I'll tell you later. There are one or two points I must clear up before I order the arrest. I'd like to drop in and have a talk with Doctor Kraus first. I believe he can furnish what little information I require."

"THIS is Mr. Peck, Doctor Kraus," Ward said as the pair entered the doctor's study ten minutes later.

"It's a pleasure," Mr. Peck conceded coolly. He drew a newspaper clipping from his pocket and handed it to Doctor Kraus. "To settle an argument, would you read this and give me your opinion?"

The doctor read the clipping through hastily.

"Why trepanning is nothing new," he scoffed. "The ancient Egyptians practiced it successfully five thousand years ago. They...."

"Never mind," Mr. Peck interrupted sharply. "I don't care a rap if the practice is new or old." He glanced sharply at Ward, who stood gaping in astonishment, then back at the doctor. "The point is, Doctor Kraus, how does it happen that you are able to read fine news print and yet, while performing autopsies on nine different corpses, you missed the fact that each of those persons had died from a shot of xetholine caniopus as was clearly indicated by the red blotches on the face of each individual victim?"

Doctor Kraus stiffened and stared at his inquisitor with cold precision.

"I'm afraid I don't quite follow you, Mr. Peck," he said smoothly.

"That likewise makes little difference. I also note that your toes point out considerably more than the toes of the average person."

"Your remark, Mr. Peck, is not alone vague, but makes no sense; at least not to me."

Ward intervened with a snort.

"You're crazy, Peck," he asserted heatedly. "I tell you I've known Doctor Kraus all my life. I'll vouch for him. I...."

Mr. Peck silenced Ward with an impatient gesture. Then turning again to Doctor Kraus, he said slowly and clearly, enunciating each word with care and precision. "There has been a murder committed, Doctor Kraus. As a matter of fact, there have been several murders, but I refer to one in particular; that of one Dominic Diaz, an escaped convict. Diaz died from xetholine caniopus poisoning. Later, his body was placed on the railroad tracks to make it appear that he had been killed by a train and to conceal the fact that he had been poisoned."

"Yes, I am aware of the incident," Doctor Kraus answered evenly. "I performed the autopsy. But...."

"And you also murdered this man, Doctor Kraus!" Mr. Peck glared into the doctor's eyes as he shot the accusation.

The old man sucked in a great breath and fell back a step and Ward saw, to his deep consternation, that the kindly light that had shown in Doctor Kraus's eyes for many a year, was no longer there.

"The tire marks that we found on the road near the scene of the train accident, Doctor Kraus," Mr. Peck continued, "were made by your car. In addition, Doctor Kraus, the poison was administered most carefully and professionally with a hypodermic needle. Only a physician, or one skilled in the use of such an instrument could so inject a poison as delicate and as deadly as xetholine caniopus. Obviously, because of the fact that you yourself were

the autopsy surgeon, and because no other person in the County is familiar with such matters, you estimated your chances of detection as being extremely small. But...."

Mr. Peck hesitated for a split fraction of a second. "Drop that!" he shouted, pouncing upon the aged physician and slapping a small glass vial from his hand.

But his action was just an instant too late, for the next moment, the old man slumped to the floor. Through eyes already dimmed by the instant action of the deadly poison, he peered up at Ward.

"I—I'm sorry, Charlie," he breathed softly as Ward dropped to his side. "After all these years, I—I've brought disgrace to—to our midst."

Ward, panic stricken and terrified, looked up at Mr. Peck, who stood frowning down at the pair.

"There's nothing we can do, Ward," he said quietly. "Look closely. The red blotches are already forming on his cheeks. Just hold him another ten seconds."

Presently Ward settled the body of the old man back to the floor. Then he rose and faced Mr. Peck.

"I can't believe it," he murmured, looking away. "I just can't believe it. I can't see why he should have done it. There wasn't any reason for it."

"Ah, but there was a reason for it," Mr. Peck asserted confidently. "Through various channels, I discovered this morning that Doctor Kraus was deeply involved financially. His circumstances were desperate. It was vitally important that he raise two thousand dollars at once."

"But I can't see how his killing anybody could have brought him any money. He...."

"You forget, Mr. Ward," Mr. Peck elucidated with a wry smile, "that Doctor Kraus was not a permanent employee of the County. He was retained, as needed, to perform an autopsy and preside at the inquest. For these services, he was paid at the rate of one hundred dollars a case. Twelve inquests at one hundred each, comes to twelve hundred dollars; or at least it did when I studied mathematics as a small boy. Now, Mr. Ward, is the motive clear?"

Ward nodded.

"The doctor needed eight hundred dollars more," Mr. Peck concluded. "But for a strange set of circumstances which brought me here, you, Mr. Ward, might have been his next victim."

DEATH IS DEAF

by
CLIFF CAMPBELL

Big Sid couldn't understand it, and he was a smart monkey. He had cased this job himself, personal. Had cooked up the scheme for pulling it off and spent a good two weeks laying the ground-work. Yet, here he was locked up in the county jail with the hot squat waiting to claim him.

BIG SID couldn't understand it. And he was a smart monkey. He had cased this job himself personal. Had cooked up the scheme for pulling it off. Had spent a good two weeks laying the groundwork. Nobody yet had ever called Big Sid Cloras a dummy either. Yet here he was locked up in their tin-can of a jail, as good as a dead duck. He couldn't understand it.

It couldn't be. Not for him, Big Sid. Yet the bars of that cell door were chrome steel, not papier mache. And those birds chatting down the hall were local coppers with a couple of men from the County

Homicide Squad. And an escort of State Troopers were en route to take him over to the real clink at the county seat. It couldn't happen to him, Big Sid. But it had. And it was going to be for murder, maybe.

"Sid....Sid," said Johnny the Itch almost reverently. He always addressed Big Sid that way. He said, "Sid, I think maybe I got something figured. But—but how did it happen, Sid?"

"Aw, shut up," said Big Sid with a disgusted glance over his thick shoulder. He didn't bother really looking at him. Nobody much ever had bothered looking at

Johnny the Itch. He was one of those little insignificant hangdog things with vacant eyes. Round-shouldered. The kind they turn off the assembly line to hold up the fronts of pool parlors. He had that twitching muscle in his right cheek. It made the skin jerk and pull as if he were trying to get rid of an itch without using his hand. He could do one thing. He could tool a heap like a maniacal genius born with a steering wheel in his hands.

"Shut up," Big Sid grunted his way again and walked past the bowl in the corner of the cell. He was trying to figure this out. He stood there winding the tail of his necktie around a big finger.

Johnny the Itch pulled nervously at the wide-brimmed fedora jerked down on his bony skull. "But, Sid, I think I got a way to—"

Big Sid turned around, spat out his cigaret, heeled it into the concrete. He didn't take his eyes off Johnny the Itch for a long moment. They were big muddy eyes, protruding. When Big Sid looked at you that way, a guy felt he was being measured for a casket. Big Sid could haul off and belt your teeth down your throat with those tremendous arms of his. And those eyes would never change.

He really wasn't a tall or unusually large man, Big Sid. But he was solid beef. That big belly that filled out a double-breasted drum-tight. The massive shoulders that started minus courtesy of neck from right beneath his double chin. The big, wide-nostrilled nose that gave him a certain kind of heavy dignity. He exuded bigness.

Johnny the Itch fingered away sweat that rolled down from under his fedora and nodded obediently. He felt of the fedora gingerly as Big Sid turned away. Big Sid was thinking and had to be let alone. When Big Sid thought, it was real important. Later, he'd tell him.

Big Sid sweated and listened to the buzz of voices from down the corridor and tried not to believe he might have signed his own death warrant. He put his hands on his broad hips, ignoring the bandaged wrist where that copper's bullet had got him. He went back to the beginning.

It had been such a sweet set-up. This dinky little whistle-stop of a town. Duffyville. Over near the southwestern border of the state. With its single bank, the Duffyville National. And that motor parts plant on the outskirts with its heavy back-log of defense orders that had compelled a doubling of its help. A consequent raise in its payroll, too. And that payroll moved through the bank, naturally. Just a little matter of something over $21,000 each week.

"It's a shame to take it," he, Big Sid, had said in the beginning. Then he had cased it thoroughly. And he had moved into town, openly and aboveboard. Registered at the little hotel as one "Samuel Norris." Big front with plenty of credentials and a neat black mustache which could be shaved off easily enough later. Then he had walked right into that bank and identified himself. Even opened up a small checking account. "Just for ready cash, of course."

That was the way he did things. Cool and nervy. Always thinking, thinking ahead. He was a smart guy. Sure maybe you could grab that dough by blasting your way with the heaters plenty. But that kind of stuff only made you hot as hell, afterward. You had to keep lamming and maybe you never got a chance to enjoy it. Big Sid wasn't dumb like that.

His way, it had been a cinch to get the whole layout. How the payroll cash was brought from up the line in an armored car to the bank before opening time in the morning. And the company guards came down and picked it up immediately after lunch for their auditing department. After lunch!

He had put his finger on that weak spot almost from the start. The quiet lunch-hour in a sleepy little town. When two of the tellers and the bank officers went home to eat the way they did in those hick burgs. That was the time for the snatch.

And even that was not to be done crudely. Not Big Sid's way. He was pretty well known in the Duffyville National by then. Been dropping in to confer with the vice-president about the local real estate situation. It was so simple. A few hints dropped about the possible establishment of a new branch plant....of course, a man wasn't always free to mention in advance whom he represented. And they'd have to get definite word about the extension of a railroad siding for the lading purposes, too.

Oh, it went over big. He knew how they did things in that bank. And he made them feel they knew him. Which was very important. Especially that teller down at the end window, Eckland. The one who stayed when the others went out to eat at the noon hour. Eckland was sort of good looking in a weak blond way. He studied accounting at night. "Samuel Norris" said he might know of an opening for a bright young fellow there. When he came up to the city, they'd have to get together. Least he could do would be to show him around the hot spots some night. That always made Eckland flush some; you could see he was the type who dreamed of himself as a glamor boy, a killer-diller with the dames.

And there was that fallen-arched Paddy who was the guard. Nice and simple. An occasional cigar, a friendly slap on the back, did for him.

So there she was. Perfect. The clincher was to get away without firing a shot. Before there was a warning. No shooting and they would be miles away before they stopped rubbing their eyes in that one water-tank burg. Probably wouldn't have figured out exactly what had happened until some time Saturday. The payroll came in on Friday.

They scoured every main artery and side road and cart track for miles in every direction, he and Johnny the Itch. They figured on cutoffs in case of a chase and how they could double in their tracks. And the pass over the mountain ridge that would take them across the state line. And about forty miles down the line, on that abandoned farm, they located the old barn where they would switch cars. They would hide the second heap in the barn. Williams would take care of that. He as the trigger man. Sonny Williams, cool as ice behind the business end of a Tommy gun.

Now, Sonny Williams was—

"Sid," Johnny the Itch said, watching the cell door nervously. He couldn't keep the whimper out of his voice now. "Sid, time's getting short. I—I think I got a way, a chance for us anyways. I got something—" His whisper cracked and he made a faint gesture toward his fedora as if he feared the walls had eyes as well as ears.

He was scared as hell. It made Big Sid sick. The little rat didn't have anything to be scared about. Not like he did. He glared at him. "I'm thinking," he warned heavily.

Johnny the Itch nodded so his under jaw jiggled. When a phone jangled down the corridor, his eyes bugged right at the door. Then he couldn't stand it any longer. "Look, Sid, how did it happen? You're smart. You figured it all out and—" He half choked and had to dredge his voice up out of his throat again. He took his hat carefully by both hands. "Look, Sid, I got—"

Big Sid took him by a bony shoulder and threw him. Back over the lower bunk of the cell. Johnny's head bounced off the wall. One of the town flatfoots came down and stared in, chewing gum methodically. He gave barely a glance to Johnny the Itch. The latter crouched there, frozen, hanging onto his hat as if it were a hunk of dynamite.

L IGHTING a fresh cigaret, Big Sid paid no attention to the copper. He was thinking what to do. He pulled at a vest button and picked up the thread again. She had been all set. He had given the office to Sonny Williams. Williams had planted the second heap at the old barn and they had picked him up and rolled into Duffyville. Right on the nose. At 12.08 according to his wrist watch. Dropped off Williams on that residential street around the corner from the bank.

Swung around the block. The timing was perfection. He, Big Sid, went up the bank steps as Williams came along less than ten yards away. Williams with that long bundle under his arm that looked like a florist's box. The sub-machine gun was in that box.

A local tradesman was just leaving the bank, nodded to "Mr. Norris." Then he, Big Sid, was over dropping his left hand on that guard's arm, asking affably for the vice-president. He had left for lunch, of course. And Sid slid the automatic from his side pocket and tucked it in the guard's side.

"This is a stick-up, stupid. . . . Keep your pants on an' don't try to be a hero. Now, pass me through!"

The guard's lips fell loosely away from his plates. He twisted his eyes over toward Williams. Williams was at a desk, the florist box lying in front of him, scribbling on a deposit slip. But Williams knew what was going on. The guard nodded his head on the fear-stiffened hinge of his neck and looked down at Eckland in the far cage, the only teller on now. The guard pointed toward the electrically controlled door in the teller cage partition that cut off the offices and vault from the customers' side.

Eckland was looking down, smiling at "Mr. Norris." Eckland nodded. He pressed a button in his cage. The door down the line clicked. And he, Big Sid, was through, inside. It went smooth as grease.

Williams was over, the Tommy gun out. Had herded the guard into a corner where he was hidden from the teller as well as any passersby. Behind the partition, he, Big Sid, wasted only a single glance at the open vault. That would have been the stupid move. He was too smart for that. He moved swiftly down behind the empty cages toward Eckland's, walking on his toes. His left foot hit a discarded paper bill binder and it crackled and he pulled away from it so he struck one of those adding machines on a portable carriage. It jolted and rattled loudly. But Eckland did not look around.

Then he was right behind him. Had the automatic snout poking through the steel grille of the rear of the cage. Square at Eckland's back. Smack at the belt of his pinchback coat. "This is a stick-up, Eckland," he said quietly. "Don't try to be a hero—or I'll blow you outa your shoes!"

There was no sign from Eckland. He stood motionless, writing hand poised over a voucher.

"Now you're showing sense," he congratulated Eckland. "Now back up easy and unhook this—"

There was a low whistle. That would be Williams. It meant a depositor had come in. Williams had moved around to cover him with the Tommy gun. And that meant Eckland could see him and the gun now. Eckland's jaw unhinged and the pencil slid from his limp hand and fell to the floor. He peered forward, making gagging sounds.

"I told you this was a stick-up," he, Big Sid, told him, speaking louder now. "I got a gun on your back! Make a move for that alarm and I'll give it to you! I'm not fooling, Eckland!"

There was a long second ticking off into eternity. That Eckland almost acted as if he didn't hear. His head never even started to twitch toward the rear. One of his hands clawed at the counter in front of him. Then he was moving. His right leg. Shakily but purposefully. Toward that pedal that sounded the hold-up alarm, flashing it right to local police headquarters.

"Eckland, I'll kill—" But Eckland's foot never halted. And he, Big Sid, let him have it in the back. Twice point-blank.

But even as he tumbled, buckling forward in the middle, twisting with agony, Eckland's foot found the pedal, punched it. The damage was done. The bank resounded with the strident clamor of the gong. And Big Sid knew its twin was galvanizing them down at police headquarters.

He ran for it. Was moving even before the teller's slumping body hit the floor. Got through the partition door; he had even thought to block the snap-lock with a paper wad. Williams was out, going down the steps. The Tommy began to chatter. Then it was clattering down on the sidewalk, Williams crumpling over it with two slugs in his body. That cop coming out of the hardware store down the block happened to be a crack shot.

He, Big Sid, had sent him scurrying back with one well-aimed slug though. Then headed for the car parked down beyond the "No Parking" zone directly in front of the bank. He always believed in keeping the law when nothing was to be gained in breaking it. He was smart that way.

It was the cop running from across the street who got him in the wrist and made him lose the automatic. A lucky shot. Still, he might have made it. He got the car between them. He was almost at it, lunging for that open front door on the curb side. Johnny the Itch was quaking in there behind the wheel, hands up at his ears, yapping, "Cripes, I give up—I give up!"

Big Sid had always known how yellow Johnny was. That didn't bother him. He could take care of him when he got inside, got to that stubby .38 he had slipped into the glove compartment just in case. But he never got to it. That police car, roaring up from behind, siren a-scream, smashed into the tail end of their job. Jolted it ahead savagely. And with one foot on the running board, he was slammed to the ground hard, rolling his head against a tree. Then they had him. Him and Johnny the Itch. Only Johnny didn't count.

BIG SID shook his head. He still couldn't figure how it had happened. It was crazy, that guy, Eckland, committing suicide like that. Something had gone wrong but—

Johnny the Itch crept closer across the

cell to Big Sid, shooting nervous glances toward the door. He admired Big Sid tremendously. Big Sid was so plenty smart, not a dumb cluck like him. He didn't blame Big Sid for what had happened. It *couldn't* be his fault; Big Sid never made a mistake. He could think.

Maybe he had figured out what had gone wrong by now. He would ask him, then tell him what he had. It was dangerous to interrupt him when he was thinking. But time was growing short. And then when he knew, Big Sid would figure out a way to use it. Johnny put a hand to his jammed-down hat and spoke.

"Sid, you got it figured how we was double-crossed maybe? What slipped? I know *you* figured it right." His voice squeaked out of his throat. "But—Sid, I got something you can figure on now, maybe. I got—"

Big Sid whirled on him, one of his heavy hands sweeping. He batted Johnny the Itch's fedora onto the side of his head. Johnny clutched at it as if it might be a life preserver. He started: "Sid, I got a—"

One of the County Homicide men came to the cell door. He plucked the cold cigar from his mouth and nodded at Big Sid. "You're lucky, pal. The hospital says Eckland the teller will pull through. If he hadn't, it would have been first degree and the hot squat for you."

Big Sid sneered. "Ah-h, that dumbhead, Eckland! He wanted to be a hero. He was asking for it!" He spat disgustedly onto the floor. "If he'd had any sense, he wouldn't have gone for the alarm. I told him I had a gun in his back!"

The Homicide man shook his head. "He never heard you."

"But I was only two feet away! I told him twice an'—"

"Eckland was stone deaf, chum," the Homicide man said.

Big Sid's lips curled. As if somebody had tried to tell him a fairy story. "Why, I talked to that chump many a time! I—"

The Homicide man agreed on that one. "Yeah, facing him. So he could look at you—and your lips. Eckland was a lip-reader. And—he was stone deaf, Cloras."

Big Sid swayed. He might have pulled it off if that guy hadn't been deaf. Could have. He swore, raking his hair savagely. "I never figured on that! I never figured—"

"*You*—you never figured that?" Johnny the Itch was on his feet when he screamed. His splinter of jaw jerked out fiercely. "You—Big Sid—the smart guy! You never figured—you—you was dumb?"

But he couldn't seem to believe it. Then —he did.

He jerked off his fedora, grabbing inside it. He came out with the stubby .38 from the glove compartment. He had been able to slip it out in the excitement after the capture. Nobody ever paid much attention to Johnny the Itch. Any more than they had thought to look under his hat when they searched him.

He said it again to Big Sid. "You was dumb." Then he just kept triggering until the gun was emptied and he had put five slugs fatally into Big Sid's carcass.

Asthma Mucus Loosened First Day for Thousands

THREE GUESSES

by
DAVID
GOODIS

Detective Frey came in and saw Duggin lying dead, and he figured he'd go out and do big things. He went out and threw his weight around. Doing big things? You figure that one out!

IT WAS ONE of those white stone places up in the east seventies. Plenty of class, Frey thought as he walked up the steps. He turned and looked at the guy waiting in the car. He shrugged, and the guy shrugged back.

Frey was in his early thirties. He was five eight and he weighed 170 and it was packed in like steel. He was a private dick and he was reckless. It showed in his grey eyes and the glint in his carelessly combed light brown hair and the set of his jawline. It showed in the thin grin of his lips.

His lips grinned like that as the door opened. A servant, a Jap.

"Yes, please?"

"I'd like to see Miss Rillette."

"She busy."

"Not too busy to see me," Frey said. "I'm coming in."

Japs are either very tough or they are very timid, and the servant was of the latter stamp. He stepped aside and Frey walked through a pale orange room, then through a burnt orange room and then into another pale orange room.

"Nice place you've got here, Miss Rillette," Frey said.

She was small and slim and even in the frock of a sculptress she looked delicate and graceful. In one hand she held a chisel. In the other she held a mallet. She was working on a chunk of marble and she had the forehead and general scalp contours almost completed.

When she turned around she showed a good looking set of features. She had dark brown hair coming in bangs to the eyebrows, and her eyes were gold-hazel. Her mouth was a little too wide, but still she was a good looking girl. She was in her late twenties.

"Just who are you and what is the meaning of this?" she said.

"My name is Frey, and I'm a friend of Harry Duggin."

"Is that so?" she said. "How is Harry?"

"He's dead."

She blinked a few times and then she said, "What happened—and when?"

Frey said, "He was murdered—this morning. Knifed."

She blinked a few more times and then she looked at the floor for a few seconds. Frey was watching her and then he was glancing sideways to a little jade box that held cigarettes. He took one up, eased a stray safety match from his vest pocket, flicked it with his fingernail, and lit up.

He took a few deep drags and said, "I got an idea that you know something, Miss Rillette."

Her face showed no emotion as she said, "I thought you said you were a friend of Harry's. You sound more like a detective."

"That's right. Harry was a good friend of mine. We went to law school together. He became a successful corporation lawyer and I starved for a while and then I became a private detective. I lost touch with Harry for a year or so and then last week he called me up and asked me to do a favor for him. He asked me to follow you."

She said, "Indeed?"

"That's right. He must have been looking around for a private dick and then he found out that I was in business and he asked me to follow you. He said that in return for the favor he would give me one hundred and fifty bucks. So you see, Miss Rillette, I have nothing against you personally. I just have to make a living, that's all."

"Why did he want you to follow me?"

"You don't have to ask me that, Miss Rillette. You know the answer. In fact, you know all the answers. I found that out through seven days of following you."

She blinked some more and then she reached out to the little jade box and took a cigarette. Frey flicked one of his safety matches with his fingernail and gave her a light.

"What am I supposed to say?" she murmured.

He knew he was going to have trouble with this girl.

"You don't have to say anything. I'll write out a confession outline and you sign it. If you want to, you can fill all the gaps. But what I want most is a signed confession—"

"What did you say you were?" she murmured.

"A private detective."

"Beginner, aren't you?"

That made him sort of sore. But he swallowed it and said, "Maybe, but I'm not an amateur. I make a living out of this."

She blinked and dragged half-heartedly at the cigarette and then she turned and looked at the marble she was doing. She looked back at Frey and her eyes were tired as she said, "How close did you follow me?"

"Here's what you did," Frey said. "On Sunday you attended an exhibition at the Wheye Galleries, up on 57th Street. From there you went to Larry's, in the Village, where you had a dinner engagement with a man named Lasseroe. From there this guy took you to a party at the Vanderbilt. He went home alone. You stayed at the Vanderbilt. You stayed there for five days, with your very good friend, Daisy Hennifer, the jewelry designer. You had a few luncheon and dinner engagements with Lasseroe. You went to a few shops with Daisy. Then early last night you left the Vanderbilt and I lost you in Fifth Avenue traffic. I went back to tell Harry about it and to get your home address, because in all the days I'd been following you—well, you didn't once touch home. When I got to Harry's apartment, his valet informed me that Harry was out for the evening."

"That's as far as you got?"

"Hardly. I went to Harry's apartment again this morning. The valet came to the door and told me that Mr. Duggin was sleeping. I explained that it was certainly most important and I went in. But I couldn't wake Harry up, because he was dead. I don't know why I'm telling you all this. You know it already."

"How did you get my home address?" She was still blinking a lot, but she wasn't excited.

"The valet gave it to me."

"You told him—?"

"I didn't tell him' anything. I came out of the bedroom and told him that Mr. Duggin was still sleeping. Then I asked him for your address. Maybe he still thinks that Harry is asleep. Or maybe he's found out already and the police are in on the case."

She looked at the ceiling and then she looked at the floor and then she looked at Frey and said, "Now let me understand this. You say that I murdered Harry. You want me to sign a confession."

"That's all there is to it," he said.

"You're going to place yourself in a lot of difficulty," Mr. Frey," she murmured. "I advise that you give this matter a little more thought before you accuse anyone else—"

"I'm not accusing anyone else," Frey said. "What are you going to do?"

She blinked and then she looked at her wrist watch and then she looked at the marble. "I have a lot of work to finish before three thirty this afternoon," she said. "Please go now."

She turned, took up her mallet and chisel, and started to work on the marble. She acted as if Frey had already walked out of the pale orange room.

He shrugged and walked out.

The Jap servant followed him to the door. He said to the Jap, "Tell Miss Rillette that I'll be back—after three thirty."

He walked down the steps and stepped into the parked coupe.

He turned the key in the ignition lock and said, "No go."

"What happened?" this other guy said. This other guy was Mogin. He was about as tall as Frey and he weighed a little over 200 pounds. He had close-cropped blond hair and pretty blue eyes and he was a very tough boy.

"She don't know from nothing," Frey said. He took the car around the corner and stepped on the gas.

"What do we do now?" Mogin said.

"Well, we could go to a double feature and kill the afternoon that way. Or we could go up and visit this Lasseroe."

Mogin shrugged.

IT WAS a new apartment house near Morningside Heights. It was elegant and smooth and important.

"Do I wait?" Mogin said.

"Maybe you better come in with me."

They went in and rang Lasseroe's number and he must have been expecting somebody because he buzzed an answer right away and the door opened. When Frey and Mogin stepped out of the elevator, Lasseroe was standing at the door of his apartment and when he saw them he expected them to walk right by. But they came up to him.

He was a man of medium height and he had a good build for a man of. forty-five. He had a square, rigid-boned face, and deep-set dark grey eyes, and a good head of black hair threaded with silver. He was wearing a long collared silk shirt and an expensive cravat and an expensive silk lounging robe.

"Hello, Lasseroe," Frey said.

"I beg your pardon—"

"You don't have to beg anybody's pardon," Frey said. "All you have to do is answer a few questions. If you don't mind we won't waste time out here in the hall. We'll go into your room and talk."

"I presume you are thieves?" Lasseroe said. He wasn't excited.

"No, we ain't thieves and we don't like funny boys," Mogin said.

Lasseroe walked into the apartment and Frey and Mogin followed.

"Now, gentlemen?"

"My name is Frey. This is my assistant, Mr. Mogin."

Lasseroe ignored Mogin. He said, "What do you want with me?"

Frey began to talk. He didn't look at Lasseroe. He looked out the window and talked slowly, taking his time. He said, "You got a nice business, Mr. Lasseroe. You are an expert appraiser of art, and you take good fees from various dealers. Sometimes you hit healthy money. You check up on a Rembrandt and you give your okay to a buyer and the dealer gives you a sweet kick-back. It is all very legitimate and lucrative—"

"What are you, a census taker?" Lasseroe said.

"Quiet," Mogin toned.

"A short time ago you figured out a few new angles," Frey said. "You weren't doing so good on the old stuff and you reasoned that you might be able to make up for the deficiency by a few transactions with the modern boys and girls."

"Just what do you mean by—"

"Quiet," Mogin toned.

"So here's what you did," Frey said. "You rounded up several of the more snooty painters and sculptors—the artistic boys and girls who have a lot of dough because their parents or some uncle or somebody had a lot of dough. You told the suckers that you'd boost their work in return for tribute. Then you went to the dealers and told them that you had several sensational new artists whose work would bring high prices. You'd give that work a big build-up in return for the kick-backs. It worked."

"Now just a moment—"

"Quiet," Mogin toned.

"Everybody was happy," Frey said, "because nobody really lost out. The artists made dough and the dealers made dough and the customers thought they were getting high class stuff. One of these customers was Harry Duggin, the successful corporation lawyer."

Lasseroe opened his mouth to say something. Then he closed it and looked at Frey and looked at Mogin and looked at Frey again.

"You sold Duggin a few pieces of sculpture done by a girl named Tess Rillette," Frey said. "Duggin liked the sculpture and he wanted to meet the girl. You introduced him to Tess and he went crazy. He worshipped her. He asked her to marry him. She thought it was funny and she told you about it. You didn't think it was funny. You saw a new dodge—"

"Now damn you—"

"Quiet," Mogin toned.

"Duggin was out of his head because of Tess Rillette. And of course he bought up every piece of sculpture that Tess turned out. This sort of thing went on for more than a year, and Harry didn't know that sculpture takes a long time and a high-class artist can turn out so many pieces and no more in a certain period. In other words, Harry didn't stop to figure that you were selling him stuff that Tess Rillette had nothing to do with. That is—he didn't stop to figure about it until he found out that Tess had fallen for you."

"Now you look here—"

"Quiet," Mogin toned.

"Harry could be clever when he wanted to be, and he was always clever when he was good and burned up. He checked up on that stuff you sold him, found out that it was phoney. He got in touch with you, told you that you were slated for jail—but that you could snake your way out of it—by giving up those happy little plans for yourself and Tess Rillette. By that time, you were serious about Tess and you wouldn't give her up for anything. So you went and murdered Harry Duggin."

"What?"

"I said—you murdered Harry Duggin."

Lasseroe stared at the lavender rug. He raised his eyes and said, "Is Harry—dead?"

Frey reached in his pocket and pulled out a safety match and flicked it with his fingernail. Then he remembered he had no cigarette in his mouth and he reached out and Mogin took out a pack and gave him one. He lit the cigarette and he said, "I'm a detective, Lasseroe. I'd like you to tell me how you did it."

"I didn't do it."

"No?" Frey looked at Mogin. Mogin shrugged.

"No, I didn't do it," Lasseroe said. "Let me see your badge."

"I don't have a badge. I'm a private detective."

Lasseroe said, "I've a good mind to call the police."

"You don't have to call them," Frey said. "They'll be here soon anyway." He walked to the door. Mogin followed.

Lasseroe stood there in the center of the lavender rug. He said, "You gentlemen have wasted your time."

"Quiet," Mogin toned.

In the elevator Frey said, "Maybe we can still make that double feature."

"I'm getting hungry," Mogin said. "How about some lunch?"

Frey parted his lips and the cigarette fell from his mouth. He stepped on the stub and said, "We'll have lunch and then we'll visit another party."

"No double feature?" Mogin said.

"No double feature. We'll visit this third party and if we strike out we'd better leave town for a few days to avoid a lot of aggravation. See what I mean?"

"I see what you mean," Mogin said. "Who do we see now?"

"We see Daisy Hennifer, the jewelry designer," Frey said. "We go to the Vanderbilt Hotel."

THEY FAKED a story that they were representatives of a big Manhattan lapidary. That got them up to Daisy Hennifer's suite. It was topaz yellow, ceiling, walls, rugs and furniture—all topaz yellow. Daisy had on a topaz yellow gown and she had topaz yellow hair.

"You won't be able to stay long, gentlemen," she said. "I've a cocktail engagement at hof post threh—"

"What's that again?" Mogin said.

"Skip it," Frey said.

Daisy was frowning.

"What did you do last night, Miss Hennifer?" Frey said.

Her topaz eyes started to glow and she said, "Just what do you mean by coming up here and—"

"Don't get excited, Miss Hennifer. We're just doing our job, that's all."

"But you said you were—"

"No, we don't represent a lapidary. We're just up here to ask you a few questions, that's all."

"You're not police—" She was wearing four rings and she was twisting them about her fingers. They were all big yellow topaz stones.

"Not exactly—" Frey said.

"Well then—"

"Do you know Harry Duggin?" Frey said.

"Why—yes. In fact, I was to see him this afternoon—"

"You won't see him, Miss Hennifer," Frey said. "He was murdered this morning."

"Oh—"

"He was a fine sort, Miss Hennifer. You shouldn't have done it."

"Done what?"

"Killed him."

She was twisting the topaz rings. They circled fast about her long fingers, the nails of which held topaz yellow polish.

"You've been friends with Harry for a long time, Miss Hennifer," Frey said. "As far as you were concerned, it was more than friendship. You went for Harry. But he wasn't serious. And he finally gave you up altogether because he was getting big ideas concerning Tess Rillette. You hated Tess. You had known her for some time and you had paid no particular attention to her, except to laugh behind her back. You looked upon her as a girl with a lot of money and no brains and no real ability as a sculptress. When you saw her at teas and parties you just saw her, that was all. But when Harry fell for her, you had to pay attention, and you hated her. You—"

"How do you know this? Who are you? What—?"

"Please be quiet and listen," Mogin droned.

"It was sort of natural that you should begin to cultivate this Tess Rillette's friendship. You wanted to talk to her about Harry. You wanted to find out just how much she cared for the guy. And then you found out that she didn't go for him at all. She adored another man. That made you hate Harry. But at the same time you still weren't giving up hope. You went to Harry, told him that Tess Rillette was after another man. You begged him to marry you. But instead of helping the situation, your visit made things worse. Harry began to look into the matter. He found out about Tess and this man Lasseroe. He wanted to make doubly sure. He was worried about a lot of things. He had a private investigator follow Tess around during this past week."

Mogin threw a cigarette. Frey caught it and flicked a safety match with his fingernail.

Daisy Hennifer was saying, "All this—it's—I don't know what to think. I don't know what to say."

"You don't have to say anything," Frey said. "Just write me a confession note, that's all. Just write out the confession and sign it and you won't have to say anything."

"But—but—"

"It was convenient for you, Miss Hennifer. Lasseroe had a good motive for killing Duggin. So did Tess Rillette. At first she was indifferent to Harry. And after he threatened to have Lasseroe jailed, she hated him. But your feelings were even stronger. It was your kind of hate that turned to murder."

"You're wrong," she said. She was excited. "I didn't do it."

"A confession will get you off easy."

"I'm not signing any confession," she said. "I didn't do it. I had nothing to do with it. I adored Harry. I—"

"You'll save yourself a lot of misery—"

She started to sob. "I didn't do it. I—"

Frey looked at Mogin. The short, heavy guy shrugged.

"Is that all, Miss Hennifer?" Frey asked.

"That's all I've got to say." She stopped sobbing. Her topaz eyes were dull now. "Are you going to take me away?"

Frey shook his head. "We can't take you away. We're not cops."

She stared. "Then—what are you?"

Frey shrugged. "Maybe we're just a couple of damn fools."

He nodded to Mogin. They went out of Daisy Hennifer's suite.

THEY WERE walking toward the coupe. Mogin was saying, "It's almost three."

"We'll have something to eat and we'll go back and sit in the coupe and wait a while," Frey said. He put his hand in his change pocket and took out two half dollars, three quarters, six dimes, four nickels. "We'll eat a classy lunch on this," he said. "Then we'll wait around for a little while and we'll see where Daisy Hennifer goes."

"It's all right with me," Mogin said. "Anything's all right with me—as long as we eat."

They lunched at the hotel and then they walked out to the lobby and sat down and smoked. At twenty past three, Daisy Hennifer walked through the lobby and Frey and Mogin took their time and followed her.

A cab was waiting at the curb and Daisy got in.

The coupe followed.

Up Fourth avenue and two turns to blade through heavy uptown traffic and then down the street where Tess Rillette lived. The cab stopped outside the white stone house and Daisy got out.

The coupe went once around the block and then Frey parked it at the corner.

"This looks good," he said.

Mogin nodded.

Frey said, "Maybe you better wait here. If I'm not out in thirty minutes maybe you better come in and see what's happened to me."

Mogin said, "Maybe you better take this." He reached in his coat pocket and pulled out a little pistol. Frey looked at it and made a face.

"I hate to use those things."

He took the pistol and put it in his pocket and walked up the white stone steps. The Jap came to the door and Frey said,

"Well—it's past three thirty. Miss Rillette is expecting me, isn't she—?"

The Jap shook his head. "Miss Rillette is busy. You must call later."

"Tell Miss Rillette that I—" He braked his tongue and said, "No—don't tell Miss Rillette anything. In fact—maybe you better take a walk around the block."

The Jap started to get excited. He said, "You were not among those invited—"

"Take a walk around the block," Frey said. "Look, I'll help you down the steps—" He grabbed hold of the Jap and hustled him down the steps. Mogin saw the deal and opened the door of the coupe. Frey pushed the Jap inside.

"What's this?" Mogin said.

"A glimpse of the Far East," Frey murmured. "Take him to a show. Take him to a dance. I don't care what you do with him, only keep him away from the house for a while. He'll get in my way otherwise."

The Jap started to yell.

"Tag him," Frey said. He looked up and down the street and he saw that it was all right. Then he heard a click and he saw Mogin's fist bouncing away from the Jap's chin. The Jap went to sleep.

"I'll drive around the block a few times," Mogin said.

Frey went up the steps again and took his time going through the pale orange room, the burnt orange room. Then he was moving slowly and very quietly as he heard voices coming from the other pale orange room. The orange door was closed but Frey managed to get in a look through the side windows of the studio. The windows were slits of glass running from the floor to the ceiling, and through them Frey saw Tess Rillette and Lasseroe and Daisy Hennifer.

They were all talking at once and at first their voices were low but then they started to argue and Frey got in on it.

"Clever, weren't you, Daisy?" Tess Rillette was saying. "You asked me to be your guest at the hotel, and I thought it was hospitality. But what you really wanted was to keep me away from here. You didn't want Harry to get in touch with me."

"That's a lie," Daisy said. "I asked you to stay at the hotel purely for business reasons. I wanted you to work on those inlaid ivories—"

"That's what I thought—at first," Tess

Rillette said. "But I know the truth now. You wanted to keep me away from Harry. You thought maybe you had one last chance of winning him back. And when you found out it was futile—you killed him!"

"She's right, Daisy," Lasseroe said. "You killed Harry Duggin. You worshipped him —and hated him!"

He got out of the chair and pointed at her, and a few glasses on a cocktail tray tipped over.

Daisy was shouting, "You're both lying! You're trying to place the blame on me and switch things around so that I'll be put out of the way. You're trying to commit— double murder!"

"Just what do you mean by that?" Lasseroe said.

Daisy's voice was lowered as she stared at the art appraiser and said, "You killed him. You had every reason to kill him, and you did it. And now you're trying to get me out of the way. I know the truth about you, Lasseroe. I know how you've been swindling art patrons, charging them exorbitant prices for cheap junk such as Tess puts out—"

Tess Rillette wasn't taking this sitting down. She started to call Daisy a lot of nasty names. It was all very unpleasant.

And then Lasseroe said, "You've got a lot of influence around this town, haven't you, Daisy?"

She liked that. She nodded. And there was a mean smile on her lips. Lasseroe was moving slowly toward her, and his face was pale. There was a light in the man's eyes that told Frey a lot of things. Frey reached into his coat pocket and touched the revolver to make sure that it was still there.

"You've got a lot of mouth, too," Lasseroe was saying.

"Just what do you mean by that?" Daisy looked at him straight.

"You may turn out to be quite an annoyance," Lasseroe said. He kept moving toward her.

Tess Rillette was grabbing Lasseroe's arm, saying, "Please—enough has already happened—"

But Lasseroe was excited and he was pushing Tess Rillette away and then he was making a grab for Daisy. She fell backward and he went over with her and he got his fingers around her throat. She managed to scream once and then she started to gurgle. Frey opened the door and took out

his revolver and pointed it at Lasseroe's spine.

"All right," he said, "Let's stop playing."

But Lasseroe was out of control now and he was choking the life out of Daisy Hennifer. He didn't seem to hear Frey, and he increased the pressure of his fingers around Daisy's windpipe. Tess Rillette was screaming and putting herself between Frey and Lasseroe, in an ungraceful try at the old martyr act.

Frey knew that he couldn't stand on ceremony. He had to break it up and break it up fast. He pushed Tess Rillette and she didn't like being pushed. She was screaming now, and she threw fingernails at his face. He let her have a slow right to the jaw and it sent her across the room, spinning.

Then he had a try at Lasseroe.

He tried to pull Lasseroe away from Daisy Hennifer, who by now was in a very bad way. But Lasseroe was a maniac now and he wanted to take the life away from the jewelry designer. Frey knew that he would have to use the revolver. He lifted it and then allowed the butt to come down and make contact with Lasseroe's skull.

Lasseroe went to sleep.

"WE'LL TAKE them all down to Harry's apartment," Frey said. "If the cops aren't there already, it'll be a good idea to finish the case right on the spot where it started."

"That's a very good idea," Mogin said. "I have a hunch that this will put us on the map."

Frey nodded. He prodded Lasseroe with the revolver and said, "You and Miss Rillette will sit in the opera seats with me. Miss Hennifer will ride in front." He touched the shivering Jap on the elbow and said, "The studio is in quite a bad state. Better go in there and rearrange things. If you have any questions to ask Miss Rillette, maybe you better call the police station. That'll be her temporary address before she goes away on a long trip."

He stepped into the coupe and closed the door. Lasseroe was manacled to him and Miss Rillette was manacled to Lasseroe. Daisy was still groaning as Mogin put the car in first and sent it whizzing down the street.

"You're making a big mistake," Lasseroe said.

"I wouldn't talk about making mistakes if I were you," Frey said lightly. He felt very good. All a private investigator needed was one good break like this, and he was made. The cases would come in thick and fast, and so would the dough. Frey smiled.

Tess Rillette was saying, "I told you, Mr. Frey—you were letting yourself in for a lot of difficulty, and—"

"Do I turn here?" Mogin was saying.

THERE were a few police cars in front of the high-class apartment where Harry Duggin had lived, and where he had died. The coupe parked across the street and Frey saw the crowd and the reporters. He said, "All right—here we go."

Everyone was looking and murmuring as the five of them went into the apartment house. A cop walked over and said, "What's this?"

"It's the Harry Duggin case," Frey said.

They stepped into the elevator and went up seven floors to the apartment. There were a lot of cops up there, a lot of plain clothes men and lads from the homicide bureau. Reporters and photographers and a doctor.

"What's this?" a plain clothes man said.

"It's the Harry Duggin case," Frey said.

The mob crowded around. This little deal was taking place in the living room of the apartment. The dick was saying, "Carven is in the bedroom. He's talking to Duggin's valet." He frowned at Frey and said, "What have you got?"

"Enough," Frey said. He pointed to Lasseroe. "Here's your baby. I'm going in and talk to Carven."

As he started for the bedroom door he heard Lasseroe saying, "You're making a big mistake—"

Frey smiled.

He went into the bedroom and he saw Carven, the big shot detective. He saw the two cops in there and he saw the valet, and then the corpse of Harry Duggin. Carven had the valet by the back of the neck. Carven was a big man and he was forcing the valet to look down at Harry Duggin's dead face.

Carven was saying, "Look at him. He's dead. Do you get that? He's dead. You called us in here and you figured that would automatically put you out of the picture. And you told us that a guy by the name of Frey came in here this morning and killed him. But Frey's an old pal of mine. Frey's

a private dick—a lousy one, reckless and careless, but still he's a dick and your story didn't go. You killed Duggin—why—why—?"

Not only was Carven big, he was plenty tough. He gave the valet a short left and a mean right to the ribs. The valet broke.

"I—I killed him," he said, and it turned into a sob. "I—I wanted something that he owned—"

"What was it?" Carven said. He raised his head, clipped to one of the cops, "Take this down."

The valet was sobbing, saying, "He had a fortune in little marble statues. He was always talking about those marble statues, telling me how priceless they were. He—kept talking about those statues all the time, telling me that the greatest sculptress in the world made them—and that money couldn't buy them. That's all he talked about—the statues made by Tess Rillette. He—drove it into me—made me crazy with the desire to own them. I—I—put a knife into him—"

Carven grinned. He looked at the cops and said, "Pretty fast, wasn't it? We came in on this case exactly two and a half hours ago. I can well imagine what happened to that wise guy Frey. He came in here this morning and he saw Duggin lying dead in bed and he figured he'd go out with his stooge Mogin and do big things. I'd like to see his face when he finds out—"

Then he turned and saw Frey's face.

MOGIN was talking loud and fast. He was saying, "What're you crying the blues about? It was just a bad break, that's all. And at least we pinned something on somebody. We got that smart bird Lasseroe locked up for fake art manipulations, and—"

They were walking toward the coupe. Frey was shaking his head and his head was hanging low. He said, "Can we make a late double feature?"

"Sure," Mogin said. He put his heavy hand on Frey's shoulder and said, "It's a good idea. We'll go to the movies and get it off our minds. Don't worry, pal. Better days are coming. Hey—where you goin'?"

Frey was walking away from the coupe, toward a corner drug store. "I'll be right back," he said. "I just want to go in here and take an aspirin. It'll help me wait for the better days."

THE COP WAS A COWARD
by WILBUR S. PEACOCK

Johnny Burke had the making of a fine cop in him . . . . but there was something mighty strange about Johnny Burke—something mighty strange!

I LIKED the looks of Johnny Burke the first time I saw him. He was one of the cadets who had been signed on less than six months before. He was still on the probation lists, but I could see that he had the making of a fine cop in him.

"Sergeant Southern?" he asked, when he found me in the garage, where I was wiring in a new radio, "My name's Johnny Burke, and I've been detailed to work with you in 27."

"Glad to know you, Burke," I said, coming out from underneath the dashboard of the cruiser.

We shook hands, after I had wiped some

73

of the oil from mine, and I winced a bit from the pressure of his fingers. I got my first good look at him then, and I felt my first bit of confidence since Riley, my old partner, had been detailed to the north end of the district.

He was big, and I mean big. Six feet four, he must have been, and must have weighed close to two and a quarter. Wide shoulders tapered into a narrow waist, his blond head sat squarely on his shoulders, and he carried himself with a panther-like grace. He appeared to be a swell partner to hold down the other half of cruiser 27.

I said as much, and he flushed at the compliment, which was another thing that took my liking. Too many of the cadet cops think they're big shots and are inclined to belittle the men who had been cops before they were out of three-cornered pants.

"I hope so," he said, "for I want to be a cop more than anything else in the world."

I grinned from my scant six feet. "Okay, let's see how we'll work in double harness. Shed that coat, and give me a hand with this set."

"Right," he said, and the two of us went to work.

That was our first meeting, and the one in which I judged him for the first time. I liked the kid and I let him know it, tried to put him wise to some of the things I've learned in ten years on the force. He listened to everything I said, tried to fit it in with the theories the police school had pumped into his brain. Some of it, I knew, he discarded because it didn't sound logical, but other parts seemed to make an impression on him.

He rode the other half of the seat with me for the next week, learning the neighborhood that was our patrol, memorizing names and locations and addresses as I gave them out. He learned fast, and I knew I had drawn a honey of a partner.

Still, there was something strange about him that I couldn't quite analyze. When we were alone, or when we were with the other men at one of the stations, he was big and quiet, seeming to know that he was not out of place. But when we made periodic inspections of boarding houses and the like, he was an entirely different person. He walked stiffly, his arms braced a bit at his sides. His face became a trifle white and his lips thinned, making him seem somebody suddenly alien to the kid I had for a partner. I didn't understand it, and in a way it shook my confidence in him, which, of course, meant that ours was not the instinctive partnership it should have been.

That sounds rather silly when I tell it, but there is nothing childish or amusing in its practical application. Cop teams should be as closely in accord as Tom and Jerry, or sorghum and flapjacks. The average person thinks that the mere routine of following orders takes care of the partnership angle, but that isn't the fact. Teams have to know exactly how much confidence each can place in the other, and each must know the capabilities of the other, or the two men don't make a good team.

And here was this new cadet partner of mine acting strangely as the devil any time the mere routine of covering the district became broken. I didn't like it, but I kept my mouth shut, waiting to see something definite that would prove something one way or the other.

THEN one day, down in the station gymnasium where daily calisthenics must be taken, I got my first inkling of the mental twist that was in Burke's brain.

There were half a dozen of us in the place; some of the men boxing the bags, some on the bars, and Burke and I on the wrestling mats. He and I had been practicing jiu jitsu for ten minutes, and both of us were working up a good perspiration. Neither of us had the advantage for the moment, so I went in for a quick wrist-lock and spin.

Burke straightened as I came forward, squatted and drove forward with cat-like speed. Before I knew what was happening, he had caught me with a knee catch and a hip flip, and I was skidding across the rough canvas on my face. I was growling to myself for being caught with an elementary trick, and came whipping back with my hands outspread in catch-all style.

There was blood on my face, although I didn't know it, and since I'm none too soft looking at best, I must have appeared to be rather in a mad rage at being thrown by a man of less skill than I.

I was half-crouched and gathering myself for a quick burst of energy. I noticed Burke's hands coming into position for sudden defense, and for a moment the mere fact that they were in position meant quite a bit to me. For there is no such thing as placing hands in defensive position in Jiu Jitsu; the entire science of this particular wrestling lies in keeping your hands out of the reach of your opponent.

I stopped momentarily, sudden wonder filling my mind. Burke's hands seemed to be warding off some unknown danger that was threatening, and I caught the flicker of some emotion in his grey eyes. I straightened out of my crouch, forced myself not to reveal what I had just seen.

Burke backed off a step, and slowly some of the tightness went out of his face and arms. He breathed deeply, and the sound was strangely like a gasp of relief.

"Whew!" he said relievedly, "I thought for a moment we were going to have a real fight."

I grinned, watching every play of emotion on his face, and carefully weighing every nuance in his tone of voice. And as suddenly as though somebody had told me, I knew he had a strip of yellow squarely up his back.

"That shouldn't worry you," I countered, "You could tie me into knots."

"Yeah?" he said skeptically, "And while I was tying you in knots, what would you be doing?"

I grinned, but I felt suddenly sick inside. Somehow, in the past week, I had come to think a lot of the kid. And now, despite his strength and brains and college degree, I knew that our days as partners in 27 were numbered.

I stretched, headed toward the showers, not answering his question.

"Come on," I said, "We've got just enough time for a cup of coffee before our shift."

I watched him that night and for the next three days. Now that I was particularly noticing him, I could see that my analysis was right. He was like any other cop I had ever known while in comparative safety, but when out of the usual routine and into some beer dive or fairly tough hangout, he was yellow clear to his heart.

He proved that one night when we picked up a quartet of drunks at a dive on the south end of our district. We went there on radioed orders, the complaint being phoned into headquarters by some old maid whose sleep was disturbed.

I shoved through the door of the dive, Burke following close behind. The report had been right, for we could hear the quartet murdering 'Sweet Adeline' in the back room. We went down the narrow passage and over to the drunks' table.

"Come on, fellows," I said, "we're going for a little ride."

Burke stood at my side, not saying anything, carrying himself with that same strained look that I had noticed the first few days we were together. The drunks joked with me at first, insisting that Burke and I have a drink or two with them. I wheedled with them for a while, not wanting to get tough.

And then the entire situation changed. The drunks got ugly, wanted to fight. I obliged them, taking the two on my side of the table, leaving the other two for Burke. I crossed a short right, then lifted a left, and turned to see how my partner was doing.

ONE of his own men was down, a bloody welt along the side of his head, and the other was cowering drunkenly from the heavy gun in Burke's fist. I knocked the gun up just as his finger pulled the trigger. I caught the gun from his hand, looked at his face in amazement.

"What the hell do you think you're doing, Burke," I yelled, "These men aren't criminals; they're just drunk!"

"He was going to hit me with a beer bottle."

"So what!" I was shaking with the neatness with which tragedy had almost struck. "Hell, you don't shoot a man because of that!"

"But that's what that gun's for. I'm supposed—"

I looked at the drunks, who were rapidly sobering. "Get out of here and go home," I said, then turned to Burke, "Come on, let's get out of here."

I reported over the two-way radio that a gun had been fired accidentally, in case somebody phoned in about it, also explained that the drunks had disappeared when we got to the scene of the complaint. Then I turned back to Burke who was huddled in white-faced silence in the side of the seat.

"For God's sake, Johnny," I said slowly, "Just because you're a cop and wear a badge doesn't give you the license to shoot that gun any time you get a notion."

"I know," he said miserably, "I know."

And that was all that was said that night. Burke was uncommunicative and sullen the rest of the shift, seeming to realize now just what a boner he had pulled. As for me, I still shook with horror when I remembered how close he had come to putting a slug through the drunk. I didn't say any more, even tried to apologize for his action in my mind.

I tried to cover up for him by saying that he was just a rookie and untrained. Too, I remembered how frightened I was the first time I had any trouble. I walked into a gang fight and waded into the leader of one gang. I had my man down, and was bouncing his head on the sidewalk, when other cops pulled me off. I was so scared that I didn't even know he had been unconscious for seconds. Luckily, I hadn't killed him in my unreasoning excitement.

So I covered for my new partner, and acted as though he had made but a natural mistake.

But I was only kidding myself, for two nights later, he let me down again.

It was about eleven at night, and the streets were slowly clearing of traffic, when we rode right into the center of a bank job. I was at the wheel, thinking what a swell life my girl and I were going to have when I got promoted to a detective's job. I pulled around the corner onto Harper street, and into the path of a tommy gun's fire.

We went over the curb, the tires shot to ribbons, before I had time to take a deep breath. I went sideways out of the door, grabbing my gun as I rolled on the pavement. I came up hooting at the two men who were in the touring. I heard Burke yell something from the other side of the cruiser.

And then a couple of slugs spun me like a top, and I hit the ground, having only a hazy memory of seeing Tony Flasco dodging out of the bank's door with another guy. I passed out cold, the drum of the touring's motor sounding in my ears.

I woke up once, when Burke came around the car to see how badly I was hit. I went back into blackness remembering that the flap to his belt gun was still fastened. The yellow rat hadn't even pulled his gun!

The next thing I remember was asking for a slug of whiskey and not getting it. After that, I slowly came back to earth. I hadn't been hit so badly; just bullet shock and a nicked shoulder to keep me in bed for a couple of days. Within forty eight hours, I was sitting up, and a week later I was aching to get back into harness again. True, I was still a bit muscle tender, but I figured a thing like that shouldn't be considered when a killer like Tony Flasco is running around loose.

I wouldn't see Johnny Burke in the hospital; I wanted nothing to do with him again. So, each time he tried to visit me, I had the nurse tell him I was asleep. Finally, he must have taken the hint, for he didn't come around any more.

I felt pretty badly about the kid, but I felt worse when Riley, my old partner, visited me. He came through the door of the hospital room, that map of Ireland he uses for a face ruffled up in a wide grin.

"I warned you, Southern," he said, "but you would play with the big boys. Now, look at you—your pants are ripped."

"Oh, shut up and sit down," I snapped from the wheelchair, trying not to grin, "Who the hell do you think you are—Dorothy Dix! Cripes, you've got enough slugs in you to make you rattle like a dice box!"

"My, what a nasty temper. Tch, tch, tch!"

"Okay, okay, go ahead and gloat. But first, let's hear the latest from headquarters."

AND then his face wasn't grinning, instead it grew hard like granite. He told me the details that the chief hadn't let me know, for fear that I would get worried. Suddenly, I lost all desire to joke, too.

Tony Flasco, his lieutenant Vance, another killer named Keeper, and an unidentified man were in the mob that shot me down. They had forced the bank's cashier to open the bank for them at night, had murdered the watchman and then left the cashier for dead. He had rallied enough to identify two of the men from pictures. Burke's and my stories had fitted in the other pieces.

Tony and his mob had got away with over fifty thousand in cash and an unnameable sum in bonds. They had disappeared into thin air, were evidently holing up somewhere until the heat died down. Teletype and radio had the country blanketed, but with as much money as they had they would be able to buy their way out of the country.

"So that's that," I said, "not one blasted thing to go on."

"We haven't got a thing," Riley admitted, "but the chief thinks they're holed up somewhere in town. The identification was too fast to let them get far."

"Maybe," I said, "and maybe not."

Riley hitched his chair closer, and his face wrinkled up a bit in a smile. "There's that possibility that the chief might be right, anyway Johnny thinks so."

I felt blood pressure rising in me for the first time since my transfusion. I started to tell Riley just what I thought of a cop who wouldn't even draw his gun to save his own life. And then Riley pulled the thing that gave me my second shock within a week, and somehow it hurt me more than the slugs did.

"Yeah, Johnny," he said, "he thinks the chief may be right. He's a bright kid, too, smart as they come. He should be, he's my nephew and I put him through college."

"He's—he's your nephew?" I said.

"Sure, and a swell lad; he'll go high on the force. And Southern, you'll die laughing at this—he thinks you're about the bravest cop and finest man he ever met."

Well, that clinched it; I couldn't say a thing about the kid. I knew it wasn't the right thing to do; I should have reported him the moment I got out of the hospital, but the memory of Riley's pride stopped me before I could speak. Instead, I laughed and joked with the cops at the station, and tried not to be alone with Burke. I knew that I might tell him exactly what I was thinking if he rubbed me the wrong way.

And then on the tenth day after the shooting, Tony and his mob still in hiding, I went back into 27 with Johnny Burke. To all outward appearances we must have appeared to be the same old team, but there was a difference.

I was still taped, and the bandages irritated me every time I moved. But there was an irritation in Johnny that shifting a bandage couldn't help.

He tried to make conversation, but I wasn't in the least pleasant. After a bit, he shut up and remained hunched over the wheel, his face as white and stiff as though chiselled from marble. I felt sorry for him then, but I felt a dull hatred, too. He had almost cost me my life, and might do it again if something broke.

I made a mental resolution to apply for a transfer the moment we got back to the station.

About three in the morning, there was a furtive whistle from the mouth of an alley near where we had parked for a moment. Burke grunted something, then climbed from the car. I went, too, just out of general principles.

I knew the whistler the moment I saw him. His name was Lefty something-or-other, and he was about the sneakiest stool the department had. Burke seemed to know him, for he started talking the second we were out of sight of the street.

"You found it?" he said.

"Sure, it's down the street about six blocks. They're holed up in the old warehouse." Lefty's tone was a thin, scared whisper.

Burke pulled a packet of bills from his pocket, slipped them to Lefty's skinny hand. Then the stool was gone down the darkness of the alley, and Burke was turning to me.

"One hundred bucks," he said, "but it's worth it."

"What's worth it?" I asked, but I had a hunch about what was coming.

"The information. I've had Lefty working for me for ten days. He's spotted Flasco and his men in the empty warehouse down the street."

"Well, what are we waiting for?" I snapped, "let's take them!"

I had forgotten for the moment that the cop was a coward; but Burke didn't waste a bit of time in bringing back my memory.

"Maybe we'd better call headquarters?" he said slowly.

I CAUGHT at Burke's arm with a grip so tight it hurt my fingers.

"Let me tell you something, Burke," I said, "Lefty is too ratty to trust. Before a squad could get here, he'll tip Tony Flasco off about cops coming. That's his way; he collects both ways." I let go his arm. "We'll call headquarters, sure, but meanwhile we'll see what we can do to stop those punks from leaving."

Burke's face was whiter than any man's I've ever seen. A muscle twitched in his cheek, and his hands lifted a bit.

"Look, Southern," he said, "you don't understand."

"Don't understand!" I was so filled with rage I could barely talk. "I understand only too well. You dirty yellow rat, you're a disgrace to the uniform you wear. You're afraid, afraid to meet another man on equal footing. You were afraid of me in the gym; you were afraid of the drunk in the beer joint; you were afraid of Tony's guns—and now you're afraid to try to mop up a mob that's murdered two men in cold blood." I went toward the street. "Well, by the Gods, I'm afraid too. I'm just as scared as you of getting my belly full of hot lead. But this is my job, and I intend to do it."

"Look, Southern——" He caught at my sleeve.

I shook myself free. "Look, hell! You've got a gun; why don't you use it now the way you'd have used it on a defenseless drunk!"

"That's what I'm trying—"

I swung, lifted an uppercut from my knees. Johnny Burke went down, crumpling slackly to the cement.

"That's just in case I don't come back," I snarled, "I owe you that."

And then I was running down the street.

I ducked around the first corner, ran half a block, then slipped down the alley. I was over my rage almost as soon as I was out of sight of the cruiser, and suddenly sorry for what I had done.

I knew that he would be coming to in a minute or so, and would call headquarters and report. Meanwhile, it was my job to try and hold Flasco and his mob until help arrived. I laughed suddenly without mirth; I knew that one man didn't have a Chinaman's chance of holding four men in that warehouse.

I slowed down in the fourth block, realizing how weak my trip to the hospital had made me. My head was swimming a bit, and there was a throb of pain from my side where a slug had gouged a path.

I darted down the alley, keeping under cover, watching other shadows to see if there was a lookout posted. Finally, I came to the rear of the vacant warehouse, satisfied that I had arrived unseen.

I took a look around, trying to find a sliver of light that would reveal the part of the building in which the men were hiding. Empty windows leered back at me, scabby paint seemed to rustle in the light breeze, but I couldn't find the slightest signs of life.

I leaned weakly against the wall for a moment, wondering if the tip had been on the square, knowing instinctively that it had. I leaped and caught the bottom rung of a fire escape, pulled myself up until I could get a foothold.

Then I went upward as quietly as I could. I found an unlocked window on the third floor, slipped silently through. I held my breath for a moment, wondering if I had been heard. Then, my gun in my hand, I sneaked through the darkness.

I covered the entire floor, shaking a bit in nervousness as a rat scuttled to safety. For seconds, I wondered if I might not be smarter by waiting for reinforcements.

And then my mind was made up for me.

On the floor above there was the sudden sound of voices. I went toward the stairs, climbed them slowly. My mouth was dry, and I could feel cold sweat trickling down my spine.

"Come on, come on," That was Tony's voice. "This place'll be hotter than hell in another five minutes."

I edged further up the steps, crouched with my head just below the landing. I heard steps coming my way and saw the flicker of a light. Then I stood up, lifted my gun.

"Hold it," I said, "It's the law."

There were the sounds of startled gasps behind the flashlight, then a gun barked defiantly. I crouched a bit, blasted lead at shadowy figures. I heard someone scream in agony, then a giant hand lifted me and sent me rolling down the steps.

"Got him!" That was Tony again.

I tried to move, knew that another minute and I'd never be able to move again. I stumbled to my feet, went back to the stairs. Above, I could hear the mutter of scared voices. I knew why they didn't come down; they were afraid I was playing possum.

I collapsed on the second step, was suddenly sick because of the pain in my chest. And then, the steps vibrated from a heavy weight.

I lifted my head, wanting to see what was coming. For a moment, I couldn't figure it out. Then I screamed out a warning.

BUT Johnny Burke went on up. One moment he was limned in the glow of the flashlight, then gunfire made a blasting hell of that fourth floor. I saw Johnny Burke's body jerk a bit under the impact of the slugs, but he was too big to be stopped by them.

I got to the top of the steps, not knowing how I got there, but in time to see the finish.

One man was down, probably sent there by my bullets, and another was just crumpling from a smashed skull from a savage blow of Johnny Burke's gun. A third man turned and tried to run, but Johnny's hands reached out and hurled him against a wall. He was spreadeagled there for a moment, then slumped sideways.

And then Johnny closed with Flasco.

He went back two steps as Tony pulled the trigger of the gun, then shook his head and started forward again. He caught Tony, and they fought silently for a second. Tony was big, but Johnny was bigger. But Johnny was carrying enough lead to kill the average man.

Tony knew that and fought with the viciousness of a cornered rat. But he was no match for the devil that was Johnny then. Johnny caught him in arms like heavy lengths of hawser, and the back of his coat split from the sudden surge of strength that went through them.

Tony Flasco screamed then, screamed like a woman in deadly agony and fear. He pounded at Johnny Burke's face with bloody hands. Then there was the sound of a heavy stick breaking, and Tony went utterly limp.

Johnny loosened his grip, stood swaying for a moment. He was laughing, laughing with a madness that chilled my heart. He turned, tottered toward me, fell, then dragged himself along with his hands. He laughed when he saw my face in the flashlight's glow, but there was no mirth in the sounds.

"I'm yellow," he said, "yellow as hell! I've been afraid all of my life. Funny isn't it?" He choked a bit. "Then laugh, damn it, why don't you? I'm big, and big guys aren't supposed to know what fear is. So I become a cop, and for a while I think I'm learning bravery."

"Easy, Johnny, easy," I said, seeing the trickle of crimson on his lips.

"Easy, hell!" Johnny's hands clutched my shoulder. "Yeah, I was afraid of you; you were the first man who ever stood up to me. I was afraid of the drunk, too, and in my fear I almost murdered him. I

knew then that I could never carry a gun until I learned what bravery was."

"For God's sake, Johnny, shut up!" I yelled, "You'll talk yourself into a hemorrhage."

"You'll listen to me and like it."

I nodded, felt a sabre of pain in my chest where Tony's slug had blasted into me. I tried to move, couldn't, his hand was too solid on my shoulder.

"So I couldn't get by without a gun," Johnny Burke's voice was growing weaker. "So guess what I did—I took the bullets out. Yeah, I carried an empty gun, afraid that if it were loaded I'd butcher somebody. You thought I ran out on you the night of the holdup, but I didn't. I tried to tell you my gun was empty, but things happened too fast. And then tonight, after Lefty gave us this hideout location, I didn't have time to explain again. I had forgotten to bring shells for my gun, and wanted to get some before we raided this warehouse. But you slugged me and came yourself. I came to and followed you. Yeah, laugh that off, I followed you in here with a gun I could use only for a club. Sure I'm yellow, I'm yellow as hell, but I'm not such a rat I'd let you walk to certain death without lifting a hand. And don't tell me I was brave; I was still as yellow as I ever was. But I didn't have any choice. Hell, Southern, don't you think I'd like to be brave like—"

He crumpled inertly, his hand slipping from my shoulder. I don't remember much about what happened after that, but it couldn't have been much more than a minute before the cops broke in.

We've got beds in the same room, Johnny and I. He'll be here quite a bit longer than I will, but I figured maybe we'd better stick together while we're in here. After all, if you're figuring on being partners for a long time to come, there's no time like the present to make a few plans for the future.

I just caught a glimpse of his back through the silly gown he's wearing. Even partly covered by the bandages, I like it. Somehow, it still is pretty solid—too, I'm beginning to appreciate its whiteness.

THE END

STOP worrying — the true facts about SEX are frankly revealed!

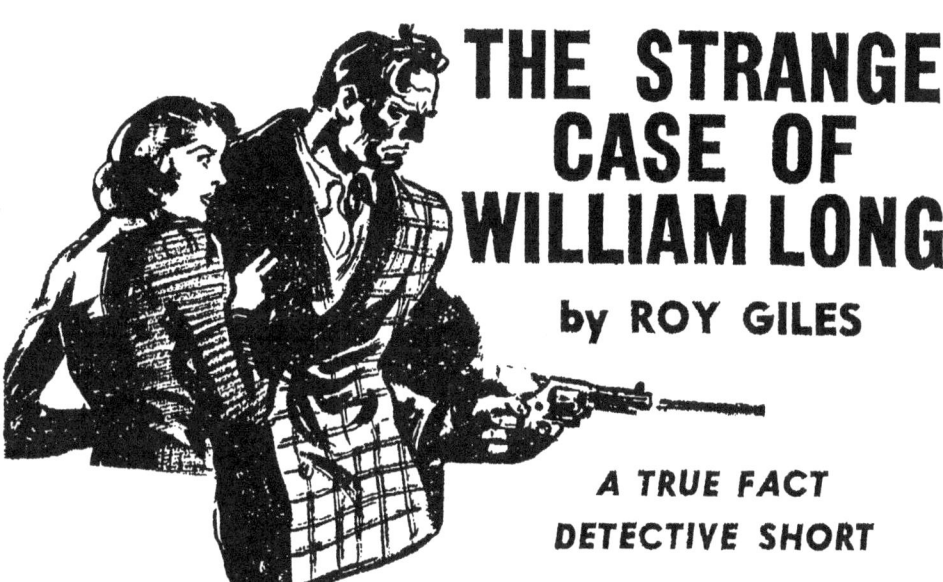

THE STRANGE CASE OF WILLIAM LONG

by ROY GILES

A TRUE FACT
DETECTIVE SHORT

AMONG the many unsolved mysteries in American crime annals the strange disappearance case of millionaire William Long, of Denver and Chicago, stands out as unusually weird. The case is doubly interesting in that it is marked by an almost exact parallel in the disappearance of millionaire William Sweet of Montreal. In each case a million dollars in cash disappeared with the victim.

So far as is known the two cases are in no way connected. It is barely possible that the same combination of kidnappers and murderers perpetrated both crimes—if they were crimes. It is not altogether impossible that both men disappeared of their own volition, although such deductions might seem highly improbable. The William Long case is the most interesting so it will be held for more detailed treatment while a brief review is given of the William Sweet case which is the more recent of the two.

William Sweet dropped from visible earthly existence in a Montreal office building a few minutes after he had been paid $1,000,000 in cash for his holdings in a Canadian theater chain. He had insisted the deal be for cash and the amount paid to him in his offices. The purchasers—according to perfectly reliable witnesses—brought the money to William Sweet's offices where they found him alone in an inner room. They paid over the money, were handed the documents of conveyance in return, and left the place. That was some twenty years ago and from that moment to now no one has ever seen or heard of William Sweet or the million dollars in cash.

His attorneys, nor anyone connected with him closely, could account for his strange actions prior to his disappearance. He was estranged from his wife. She and others were questioned long and arduously by police without result. His friends were the most mystified of all.

A few years previously William Long, one of the oddest characters ever to have existed outside the pages of fiction, dropped from sight on the street in the Loop district in Chicago in mid-afternoon. He was carrying a suitcase containing $1,000,000 in cash which he had just withdrawn from a Chicago bank. He was on his way to pay the money to the heads of a syndicate in control of Chicago's gambling concession. The money was to purchase for him a controlling interest in an illegal concession and one that would not have been regarded as

(Continued On Page 82)

Hooded Detective

(Continued From Page 81)

tangible, probably, by any man in the world except a Western gambler.

Furthermore, in order to get the million dollars with which to purchase control of Chicago's gambling institutions Long had sacrificed a perfectly legitimate and highly prosperous produce commission business. Always a gambler, Long had tumbled into the legitimate million-dollar business accidentally. He had entered into it against his better or personal judgment and had no liking for it whatever. It interfered with Long's gambling career, a situation which—to a man of Long's type—was altogether intolerable.

Western gamblers are legion—a reckless, money-plunging, romantic and venturesome yet an admittedly square-shooting clan. Long was typical of this crowd. He was a swagger dresser and more marked than many because he was strikingly handsome. Even better looking was Long's red-haired wife. They were an unusually devoted pair according to all reports.

Long was born in Chicago and even as a young man he managed to climb high in the gambling circles of that city. He was a high-ranking officer in the fabulous gambling empire of John Worth, reputed to have been the wealthiest gambler of all time with the possible exceptions of Edward Chase and Vasil Chuckovich. Chase and Chuck, as they were known, controlled all gambling from Chicago west to the coast for thirty years and amassed more than $20,000,000 apiece. Canfield, in all his glory, nor any other Eastern gambler, not even the present wealthy, staid, and conservative Col. Bradley, king of the modern gambling world, ever approached the enormous fortunes of Worth, or Chase or Chuck.

Chase was originally a Saratoga, N. Y., hotel clerk and his partner Chuck was an Austrian emigrant, kitchen worker. Both were bitten by the gambling bug in Saratoga and went West, not to grow up with, but to fairly conquer the country. They ran a dime apiece up into multi-millions without batting their eye-lashes. It was under the direction of this highly spectacular paid that William Long, a gambling genius in his own right, was destined to work in Denver.

Long left Chicago for Denver during one of those periodical municipal reform up-

The Strange Case of William Long

heavals that sent his boss, John Worth, under cover for a spell. Long arrived in Denver with his beautiful wife and a $10,000 bank roll one bright spring day at the opening of the Overland Park racing season. The Colorado resort fairly dripped with wealthy tourists and members of the sporting fraternity from everywhere. He qualified with Boss Ed Chase and was assigned territory. He opened up a rather modest gambling hall near Seventeenth and Curtis streets. This was within a stone's throw of Chase and Chuck's famous Cottage Club and it was understood that Long was to take care of the overflow from the Cottage resort.

Just to bow to a time-honored custom, the room of Long's place fronting on the street was fitted up as a fruit stand—a stall, of course, for the spacious gambling hall in the back. This was more a condescension to the church element than through any fear of the law.

Long had been in operation only a few weeks when the altogether weird began entering into his affairs. The Rocky Ford garden district in Colorado began growing small melons. Some of them found their way to Long's stall. A youth tended the stall and nobody connected with the whole establishment ever cared whether the fruit stall ever profited a dime or not. The youth knew his salary was coming from the games in back but it was customary to treat any possible stray customer for fruit quite seriously and attentively.

One afternoon Long sent the youth on an errand and took charge of the stall while the boy was gone. This was simply because all Long's dealers were doing a Monte Carlo business in back and he was the only one footloose. A man approached the stall and picked up one of the tiny cantaloupes from Rocky Ford. He cut into it with a pocket-knife and tasted the meat. Then the customer's eye-lids went up in the air. Long observed him and, as he explained later, was becoming just a little bored. Then the customer spoke, gravely, seriously:

"This," he said, "is the most perfect and the most deliciously flavored melon of its kind in all the world."

"If that's true," said Long, "nobody seems to care. I can get them at a dime apiece, wholesale. I'll sell you all you can carry at fifteen cents each."

(Continued On Page 84)

84

Hooded Detective

(Continued From Page 83)

"Where do you get them?" asked the customer.

"They're grown down in Rocky Ford," said Long.

"These melons are worth $1.50 each and I can get that for them. I'll take a trainload, laid down in Chicago, green, at fifteen cents each. I am Mr. Blank of Blank & Blank. We supply a wealthy trade, the most excellent hotels and the royal families of Europe. Wire me the market daily on these melons in season."

THAT was the beginning of the Rocky Ford cantaloupe fame. Prices soared to seventy-five cents, wholesale, within a week. Long went into the melon business with Senator Swink, of the Rocky Ford district. They bought up the entire crop and cleaned up a million dollars profit each within a few years.

Then Long became restive. The gambling germs in his blood were rampant. He sold out to Senator Swink and others and moved on to Chicago, his early stamping ground.

Worth, kingpin of the Chicago gambling fraternity, had grown old and what is known as the "concession" had fallen into other hands. Long found that, so far as the Chicago gambling situation was concerned, he was an outsider looking in. He and his wife knew that even their old friends could do nothing to change this situation.

But our hero was nothing if not a determined person. Both he and his beautiful red-haired wife liked Chicago and Long could not live without gambling, so he was put to figuring out some way to make it possible for him to fly his flags in the Loop or some other first-class commercial district.

Finally he decided that if he could gain a foothold no other way, no one would try to prevent his buying his way in. So he made his famous offer of $1,000,000 cash for a controling interest in one approved district. What happened after that might never be thoroughly understood. A little light is thrown on the shadow by some known facts regarding Chicago gamblers and their wars.

Like Long, himself, all Chicago gamblers are determined persons. The famous kill-

The Strange Case of William Long

ing of Jake Lingel and other interesting little events only go to show just how determined Chicago gamblers are at times. It is possible that there was an element in Chicago that did not exactly approve of Long's activities. It is possible that they objected to his entrance into the lists at any price.

What can happen under such conditions is shown by a page from the record which reveals that, some years back, one gambling contingent was in and another contingent was out. The outs were warring with the ins. During this one war 49 bombs were tossed and planted and 49 gambling establishments were blasted, uprooted and blown into the air.

There is no doubt that Long was aware of conditions. Whatever it was that happened to him he certainly must have walked into it with his eyes wide open.

His deal to pay $1,000,000 cash for a gambling concession progressed to a point where Long withdrew the money from a bank. He took it to his hotel room where he waited with his wife for a telephone call. The money was in a suitcase. The phone rang and according to the wife Long answered it. It was a little after one o'clock in the afternoon—broad daylight, of course.

Long turned from the phone to his wife. "I am going over now, and meet the boys," he said. "I have only got to go about two blocks and as soon as I sign up I will be right back."

"For God's sake be careful," cautioned the wife.

"Don't be silly," laughed Long. "It is broad daylight. I am only going a couple of blocks along the busiest street in the world. This suitcase will attract no more attention than any other suitcase." Long kissed his wife and left. He was confident and cheerful. But he did not come back.

The beautiful wife waited and waited. She phoned all their friends and all the hospitals.

Gamblers' wives are never in a hurry to phone the police but finally, after many hours of waiting and weeping, Mrs. Long did just that. It availed her nothing. To use a hackneyed figure, it was as though the earth had opened and swallowed her husband.

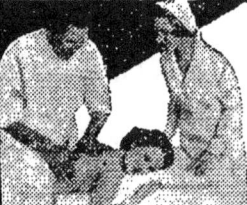

A DINNER DATE WITH MURDER
by HARRY STEIN

IT WAS long past the dinner hour and too early for the after theatre crowd. The two men at the table near the door were the only patrons in Luigi's restaurant. They had eaten and were sitting there drinking wine. They drank very slowly and it was plain that they were waiting for somebody because they weren't talking much and had the half bored, half impatient look of people who have nothing to do but wait. At a table near the back of the room the waiter, who seemed to be the only one on duty, sat smoking a black twisted cigar and reading a newspaper.

One of the men put his wine glass down and lit a cigarette. Even sitting down he was noticeably shorter than his companion but he was powerfully built. He had a deep olive complexion and eyes that were black and sparkling.

"It looks like your man isn't coming, Dan," he said.

"Don't worry about that, Gatti," Dan said. "He'll turn up. He knows the trail's hot and he'd rather be a live rat than a dead kidnapper."

Gatti shook his head slowly. "I don't know," he said vaguely. "You say you'll know if it's the same one that phoned. How can you be sure?"

"The accent. It's unmistakable. A deep voice and an accent like a vaudeville dialectician's."

Gatti refilled their glasses from the green bottle on the table. Then they were silent.

The front door opened and two men entered. One was fat with a complexion the color of old weather beaten brick and eyes that were watery and cold. He wore a high crowned, pearl grey fedora, set squarely on his head and his fleecy coat had heavily padded shoulders. The other man was slight and sallow. His coat was too tight across his back and he walked with a defiant swagger. They hung their hats and coats on the rack and sat down two tables away from the one at which Dan and Gatti were sitting. The waiter put down his cigar and came to their table, bowing slightly.

"Spaghetti wid' a meat sauce," the stout

A Dinner Date With Murder

man ordered loudly. "an' a bottle a' Chianti."

"Same," the small man said laconically.

The waiter went off without a word. The two men lit cigarettes. Dan and Gatti watched them with open curiosity, waiting for some sign but they smoked in silence, never looking in the direction of the other table.

"It's the organ grinder accent all right," Gatti said in a barely audible voice. "But where's the high sign?"

"Give him a chance," Dan mumbled. "He has to be plenty careful, I suppose."

The waiter came in with a wicker wrapped bottle which he set on the table before the newcomers. Then he went back to the kitchen and when he returned he brought two heaping plates of spaghetti, dripping reddish brown sauce and giving off a fragrant steam.

"The idea is to talk on a full stomach, I suppose," Gatti whispered. "Or isn't he the guy? I thought your man was coming alone."

"He didn't say," Dan said.

Gatti watched the fat, red faced man wielding fork and knife, eating the spaghetti with great relish.

"Dat's a pretty good a' spaghetti, eh Joe?" the fat man said loudly.

"Right," Joe replied briefly.

Dan looked toward the back of the room where the waiter was again occupied with his cigar and paper. Maybe they're waiting for the waiter to clear out first, he was thinking. He sipped at his wine, waiting. ....Then he looked up again. The stout man had almost finished what was on his plate and was taking a long drink from his wine glass. He put the glass down and sat back in his chair. He turned his watery eyes on Dan and nodded his head slowly up and down....up and down. Dan glanced quickly at Gatti who had his elbow on the table and seemed to be sleepily leaning far over to one side of his chair. Then he nodded his head at the stout man just as the latter had done.

The next instant he was on the floor and somewhere over his head, repeated claps of thunder were bursting as if they would never cease and from the other table he heard a choked scream. His ears hurt in the silence that followed.

(Continued On Page 88)

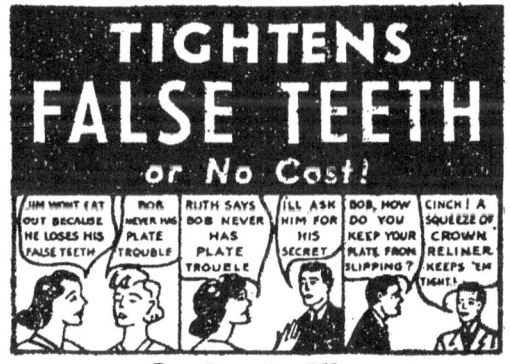

Hooded Detective

(Continued From Page 87)

WHEN he rose from the floor Gatti, gun in hand, was already standing at the side of the two men who a little while before had been enjoying their spaghetti and were now dead. The waiter had disappeared. Don took a revolver from the lifeless hand of the small, sallow faced man. He looked at the chambers. All the cartridges were neatly in place.

"He never had a chance to use it," Gatti explained.

The door opened again. A man with his hat drawn down low over his eyes, stood in the doorway and looked wildly about at the dead men and at Dan and Gatti. Then he turned around frantically.

"Our man," Gatti cried.

He leaped forward, grabbed the fleeing man by the elbow and jerked him violently into the room.

"You wanted to see us," Gatti said. "You phoned the lieutenant, didn't you?"

Every feature of the man's face was distorted with terror. Gatti shook him.

"This is the lieutenant," he said pointing to Dan. "What were you going to tell him?"

The man was looking at the corpses with a slow, steady gaze. His face was more composed now.

"Sure," he said in a deep, resonant voice. "Dey a' deada now, yes? I no hava ta be afraid, yes?"

"That's right, they're dead," Dan said. "Where have they been keeping the kid?"

The man drew a piece of paper from his pocket. Dan read the address on it and put it in his own pocket.

"Who are they?" he asked pointing to the bodies.

The man was calm now.

"Dat's a' Rocky Callahan," he said, "an'a da leetle wan he's a Joe Baker. I was a' gon' ta tell you. I was a' gon' ta—how you say—walk out on a' dem."

"Rocky Callahan from Detroit!" Dan said in surprise. "You mean the fat feller."

"Dat's a'right."

"Sucker," Gatti chuckled.

"Yeah," Dan said wryly. "But what started the target practice?"

"He pulled a rod on us," Gatti said.

"Who?"

"Joe Baker, the little guy."

"I didn't see it."

"Sure, because you weren't looking for it."

"I was looking at them."

A Dinner Date With Murder

"Baker had it under the table in the hand he wasn't eating with. You couldn't notice unless you bent down to look under the flap of their tablecloth. They must have found out their pal here was going to sing and figured he probably told us too much already. They counted on getting him later."

Dan nodded reflectively. "But what I want to know," he said, "is how you happened to be looking under their table."

Gatti chuckled some more.

"I was just making sure," he said. "Guys named Callahan shouldn't try to eat spaghetti. He might have palmed off the accent but nobody with a real accent like that would cut up his spaghetti with a knife and pick up tiny pieces on his fork."

"What's wrong with that?" Dan wanted to know.

Gatti gave him a look of contempt. "You eat spaghetti with a fork and a tablespoon to help you wind it around the fork and you eat it full length or it isn't worth eating."

"You dam' right," Gatti's prisoner put in belligerently. His fear and humility were completely gone now. "Dat's a' da only way ta eata him."

ARTISTIC MURDERS MISFIRE

A TRUE FACT CRIME SHORT
by MAT RAND

A SCIENTIFIC detective, identified with national and international law enforcement agencies, is authority for the statement that there are at least eighteen methods of murder that practically defy detection. Yet the record shows that there are very few murders committed in any one of the eighteen ways that go unpunished. In other words the old adage, "Murder Will Out," is true according to the record in about ninety percent of all felonious killings.

To commit a murder in any one of the mentioned eighteen ways it would be necessary for the murderer to be a reasonably advanced scientist. Few possess the technical knowledge necessary to destroy their fellow beings by these methods. Nevertheless, all eighteen of the methods mentioned have been tried from time to time with varying success in escaping conviction.

It would appear that persons of scientific attainment could be counted upon not to attempt murder. This is not true. Education is not a one-hundred percent deterrent to crime. Educated persons have only a slightly less average as potential murderers than the illiterate. Not even motives differ except in cases of murder for robbery. Considering robbery as greed this difference is removed. Jealousy figures as a motive in a large number of murders and among the educated murderers it is paramount.

Considering murder—for that matter all forms of crime—as an art it would seem likely that the criminals of education or scientific attainment would excel as master craftsmen. This isn't true either. Just the opposite prevails. In practically all crimes attempted by scientists they bungle their jobs completely. The record proves positively that as criminals scientists are flunkies without a single recorded exception.

Where a murder is committed by a method that destroys its own evidence or fails to leave what might be called a "trace" or clue detectives are hampered but not necessarily baffled. In these cases, almost without exception, it is circumstances that bring the criminal to punishment. While a jury might refuse to convict on circumstantial evidence a detective is not so deterred. The scientific detective turns science against the scientific murderer. He batters the suspect with circumstantial evidence until in nine out of ten cases the scientific suspect weakens and acknowledges his crime. Circumstantial evidence backed by a confession that checks on all angles is about all any jury needs to be convinced of guilt.

Artistic Murders Misfire

When your correspondent began to dig into this subject of artistic or scientific murder Government detectives—themselves master scientists—made a request. They asked that we be "a little vague" in the use of proper names and in description of the eighteen murder methods most difficult of detection. So, we will name no chemicals or poisons but confine ourselves to effects and processes.

The commonest method is the complete destruction of the corpse—the corpus delicti. Cremation is the usual means resorted to. The body is burned in a furnace or on a pyre. Effort is sometimes made to make identification impossible by burning the body or parts of it in gasoline flames. The scientist has no edge on his uneducated fellow in this type of murder case. He practically never is able to remain with the burning corpse long enough to do a perfect job.

In many cases complete dissolution of the corpse is attempted by immersion in acids. There are acids that completely dissolve bone tissue and even clothing but circumstances usually reveal these crimes. Accessibility to such chemicals and procurement of such chemicals usually lead to a search. The search usually leads to the finding of bone fragments, identifiable by means of buttons, bits of jewelry, metallic dentistry and other bits of evidence which escapes or rather resists the acid effects.

And now we get into some deep scientific water. It is actually possible by the exact and accurate dosage of a certain poison, over a long period, to produce death "by typhoid fever." This poison, a common and easily available one shows up like an electric sign when not scientifically administered. But when given in frequent and exact small quantities it produces every symptom of typhoid. Quite often the corpse is buried as a typhoid victim.

In most of these "typhoid" cases the motive is insurance and the murderer encouraged by success in one case attempts others. Sometimes there are a score of victims. In practically all cases the murderer is convicted in the long run. The circumstances

(Continued On Page 92)

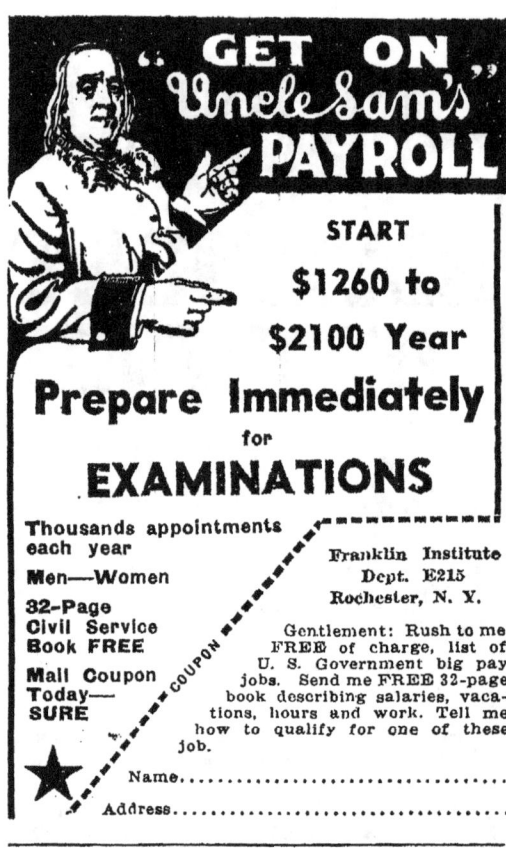

Hooded Detective

(Continued From Page 91)

that usually bring about detection are doctors and nurses and neighbors. They will remember that the murderer was always quite enthusiastic about insurance. A nurse will remember that the murderer insisted on preparing the victim's food. Sometimes a druggist will remember selling some poison to kill a dog or as an insecticide.

THERE is, too, a gas that administered in exactly correct quantities will produce "tuberculosis." This gas kills instantly unless scientifically administered. A small quantity will cause the lungs to "rot" gradually bringing death in from five to thirty days with all the symptoms of rapid or "galloping" consumption. Doctors have so diagnosed such cases but circumstances usually bring the crime to light. First among these is that the gas is rare, ordinarily. It can be home-made but only by a chemist with a well-grounded knowledge.

It would appear that, among poisons, the most powerful would be the hardest to detect. This because a small dose would leave less trace than a large one. It follows only in some cases. One very powerful poison absolutely defies detection. Another, and the most deadly poison known to man reveals itself instantly. This second poison perfumes the corpse and leaves it smelling with a fruity odor. Any doctor or chemist can identify it instantly regardless of how small the dose might have been.

In the event of the first named powerful poison—the one that defies detection—there is no odor or other discernible indication of any nature. When scientifically administered the fatal dose is less than one billionth the weight of an ordinary human body. Thus, to trace it, the autopsy doctors would have to find, separate or segregate a billionth bit of the mass under observation. The body completely absorbs the fatal chemical and so—.

This poison has its uses but is rare and impossible to obtain even by most chemists. There are few dispensing druggists who have scales sensitive enough to weigh the dosage of the chemical. Even for doc-

Artistic Murders Misfire

tors to obtain it is an undertaking involving considerable red tape. But it has been used by murderers—scientific murderers. Circumstances in these cases have proven that the murderer possessed the drug and had a motive to use it. Confession has followed circumstantial evidence in some cases and in others conviction has been obtained on expert testimony backed by positive circumstantial conditions, such as the presence of the corpse and proof of the ante-mortem possession of the fatal drug by the suspected murderer.

A fiction story of the football grid, some years ago, involved the use of a solution to produce a fatal gas under conditions of bodily heat produced by violent exercise. This was authentic so far as action and effects were concerned. In the football story the victim's sweater was soaked in a deadly solution. Under the heat of the exercise during the football game the victim's body generated the gas which he inhaled. The gas stimulated his heart action to the point where a blood vessel was ruptured causing death.

The actual case from which this fiction story was borrowed involved a man, a wife, and the wife's clandestine violinist lover. The wife knitted the sweater for her admirer. Her husband dipped it in chemical solution and dried it while his wife was absent. When she returned she expressed the sweater to her admirer. He wore it under his shirt. His body heat produced the gas which was inhaled by the violinist in sufficient quantities to cause death.

The hypodermic needle is a weapon of death which has caused autopsy physicians trouble since its invention. Murder by the hypodermic needle, no doubt, would escape detection often enough were it not for circumstances. Such circumstances of death are ever in the mind of autopsy doctors. Where evidence warrants it corpses are subjected to microscopic and meticulous search to locate a hypodermic puncture. And they can be located even when hidden back of an eyelid as was the case in one instance,

(Continued On Page 94)

Hooded Detective

(Continued From Page 93)

that of an infant. The suspected murderer, in this case, a colored mother, died in an insane asylum.

In cases such as have been described here readers might wonder why names, dates and places are not revealed. They might ask why scientific detectives desire the text to be vague. The reason is quite simple and understandable once it is explained. Even where conviction is obtained in such cases it is only after the most laborious and expensive processes and investigations. Living relatives of the accused in each case might be moved to bring suit on any of many grounds. This would result in more long, laborious and expensive litigation—to the Government, the writer, the publisher, doctors, detectives and what not?

This thing has been going on for centuries. As far back as history records mysterious poisons have been a common means of murder. There are thousands of poisons. Some of these, products of the jungles held secret by savage tribes, are still little known to or understood by scientists. Poisons are given up by the earth, secreted by plants and by animals. They are produced by combining chemicals and by chemical reactions. In nature they are begotten by elemental distillation, by the action of the sun's rays, by the excrement of animals including the fishes, by the promulgation of minute organisms, and in a myriad of mysterious ways.

Some of these processes are well understood and some little understood by man. As is the case with electrical and other forms of scientific research the field of scientific criminal detection hardly has been scratched. Research is constant and no doubt will be perpetual. No one knows where any sort of research will lead. Scientific detectives call attention to this fact:

"Such research is valuable not only in the matter of law enforcement but might prove of inestimable value in other fields. It might lead to a discovery that would end cancer or one that would end war."

don't Worry about Rupture

• Why put up with days . . . months . . . YEARS of discomfort, worry and fear? Learn now about this perfected invention for all forms of reducible rupture. Surely you keenly desire—you eagerly CRAVE to enjoy life's normal activities and pleasures once again. To work . . . to play . . . to live . . . to love . . . with the haunting Fear of Rupture banished from your thoughts! Literally *thousands* of rupture sufferers *have* entered this *Kingdom of Paradise Regained.* Why not you? Some wise man said, "Nothing is impossible in this world"—and it is true, for where others fail is where we have had our greatest success in many cases! Even doctors—thousands of them—have ordered for themselves and their patients. Unless your case is absolutely hopeless, *do not despair.* The coupon below brings our Free Rupture Book in plain envelope. Send the coupon now.

Where's YOUR Rupture?

Patented AIR-CUSHION Support Gives Nature a Chance to CLOSE the OPENING

Think of it! Here's a surprising yet simple-acting invention that permits Nature to close the opening—that holds the rupture securely but gently, day and night, at work and at play! Thousands of grateful letters express heartfelt thanks for results beyond the expectation of the writers. What is this invention—How does it work? Will it help me? Get the complete, fascinating facts on the Brooks Automatic Air Cushion Appliance—send now for *free* Rupture Book.

Cheap—Sanitary—Comfortable

Rich or poor—ANYONE can afford to buy this remarkable, LOW-PRICED rupture invention! But look out for imitations and counterfeits. The Genuine Brooks Air-Cushion Truss is never sold in stores or by agents. Your Brooks is made up, after your order is received, to fit your particular case. You buy direct at the low "maker-to-user" price. The perfected Brooks is sanitary, lightweight, inconspicuous. Has no hard pads to gouge painfully into the flesh, no stiff, punishing springs, no metal girdle to rust or corrode. It brings heavenly comfort and security—while the Automatic Air Cushion continually works, in its own, unique way, to help Nature get results! Learn what this patented invention can mean to you—send coupon quick!

C. E. BROOKS, *Inventor*

SENT ON TRIAL!

No . . . don't order a Brooks now—FIRST get the complete revealing explanation of this world-famous rupture invention. THEN decide whether you want the comfort—the freedom from fear and worry—the security—the same amazing results thousands of men, women and children have reported. They found our invention the answer to their prayers! Why can't you? And you risk nothing as the complete appliance is SENT ON TRIAL. Surely you owe it to yourself to investigate this no-risk trial. Send for the facts now—today—hurry! All correspondence strictly confidential.

FREE! Latest Rupture Book Explains All!
Sent You In Plain Envelope. Just Clip and Send Coupon ➡

Brooks Appliance Co., 119 State St., Marshall, Mich.

WILDSIDE PULP CLASSICS: PULP FACSIMILE SERIES

Series editor: John Gregory Betancourt

#1: *Spicy Mystery Stories* (August 1935)
Includes Robert Leslie Bellem, Atwater Culpepper, Ellery Watson Calder, Carl Moore, E. Hoffman Price, Arthur Wallace, and more.

#2: *Ghost Stories* (June 1931)
Stories by Conrad Richter (author of The Light in the Forest*) and E. & H. Heron featuring psychic detective, Flaxman Low.*

#3: *Spicy Mystery Stories* (February 1937)
Features Robert Leslie Bellem, Lew Merrill (Victor Rousseau) Hugh Speer, Justin Case (Hugh B. Cave), & many others!

#4: *Strange Tales #7* (January 1933)
Features Hugh B. Cave's classic "Murgunstrumm," as well as stories by Robert E. Howard, Henry S. Whitehead, and many more.

#5: *The Black Mask #2* (May 1920)
2nd issue of classic mystery mag, where hardboiled fiction was born!

#6: *Tales of Magic and Mystery* (February 1928)
Legendary rare early fantasy magazine!

#7: *The Phantom Detective #1* (February 1933)
The premiere issue of the detective-hero pulp!

#8: *Submarine Stories* (March 1930)
Rare pulp magazine, stories and articles about (what else?) subs!

#9: *Sinister Stories #1* (Feb 1940)
The first issue of this "weird menace" pulp!

#10: *The Thrill Book* (Sept. 1, 1919)
The facsimile reprint from this legendary rare pulp magazine!

#11: *The Spider* (March 1940)
Includes the *"Spider" novel* Slaves of the Laughing Death!

#12: *Spicy Adventure Stories* (Dec. 1939)
More of the classic "spicy" fiction!

#13 *Strange Tales #4* (March 1932)

#14 *The Spider #92*
Includes the "Spider" novel The Devil's Paymster!

– –

Please send me the following books, for which I enclose payment. (Or order online with a credit card at www.wildsidepress.com, or through your favorite online bookseller or pulp dealer.)

☐ *Spicy Mystery Stories* (Aug.1935) - $19.95
☐ *Ghost Stories* (June 1931) - $19.95
☐ *Spicy Mystery Stories* (Feb. 1937) - $19.95
☐ *Black Mask #2* (Jan. 1920) - $19.95
☐ *Tales of Magic & Mystery* (Feb. 1928) - $19.95
☐ *Phantom Detective #1* (Feb. 1933) - $19.95
☐ *Spicy Adventure* (Dec. 1939) - $19.95
☐ *Submarine Stories* (Mar. 1930) - $19.95
☐ *Sinister Stories* (Feb 1940) - $19.95

☐ *The Thrill Book* (Sept 1. 1919) - $19.95
☐ *The Spider* (March. 1940) - $19.95
☐ *Strange Tales #4* (Mar. 1932) - $15.00
☐ *Strange Tales #7* (Jan. 1933) - $15.00
☐ *The Spider #92* - $19.95

Name: _____

Address:_____

Address:_____

Mail to: Wildside Press
9710 Traville Gateway Dr. #234
Rockville, MD 20850

U.S. shipping: $3.95 for 1-2 books, $1 per additional book.
Other countries and online orders: see www.wildsidepress.com

www.ingramcontent.com/pod-product-compliance
Lightning Source LLC
Chambersburg PA
CBHW081157170626
46813CB00009B/3227